# Henry Wilson
## in the
# ENCHANTED FLASK

With
### CAMERON SCHULTZ

## CHRISTOPHER A. SALVO

ISBN
978-1-962868-94-5 (Paperback)
978-1-962868-95-2 (eBook)
978-1-962868-93-8 (Hardcover)

# TABLE OF CONTENTS

# ACKNOWLEDGEMENTS

I am most grateful to Cyndy Salvo, my loving wife, Sally Tedesco, a very dear friend along with assistance from her husband Michael and my sons Philip and Matthew Salvo. Each has contributed to the creation of this book.

Cyndy and Sally are credited with manuscript editing and erudite criticism and corrections. Philip is credited both with editing and helping in the creation and composition of the cover.

Matthew is the model subject in the photograph. Matthew is both a gifted and experienced surfing instructor and a custom surfboard shaper at "salvosurfboards.com" in Rincon, P.R.

# PROLOGUE

This adventure continues the episodes of **Henry Wilson Worthington** in the book "**Henry, Black Lightning and the Rubber Band**". Henry's name is too long and is shortened in the future to just Hennry Wilson. It centered about the United States' super secret agency, the **Department of Extraordinary and Super natural Events,** known in short as "**DESE**".

This agency continually investigates, as its name implies, events starting with the Area 51 extra-terrestrial crash and its survivors. It continued to develop national protection against terroristic destruction by evil, malcontented witches and demonic allies. DESE's star Federal Agent is **Mary Kent**, the director of the agency with exclusive and secret connections only to the President and Vice President of the United States.

The Area 51 incident introduced agent **Jack Henigson**, a scientist and secret agent who uncovered the extraterrestrials who changed their bodily form into **Mr. Mrazy Xilx** and the beautiful **Elizabeth Sam**. Both of these extra terrestrials became acclimated and stuck here on Earth because all of their communications and space vehicle was destroyed and beyond repair. Both became very special agents of DESE.

Henry, while a high school teenager, learned that he was endowed with extra special "gifts" and talents which border on the superhuman, extra sensory and near magical abilities.

Mary, on a vacation to Scandinavia, met up with **Seemore Manlein**, an extraordinary being. He was a Gnome. He, his wife **Hepseva**, and their very special friends, including some out of mythology, became involved in DESE activities in the dealing with evil witches.

The previous adventures dealt with evil witches, demons, black magic, voodoo and more. This earlier assignment ended in success. All members of DESE are secret federal agents, including the exceptional Henry Wilson.

The continuation of this story starts where the last escapade ended. All members of DESE may not all take part in this book, but they remain in the background as supporting Federal Agents.

This next adventure starts soon after Henry returns home. It is as though Henry really has no time to rest before this next episode begins with an extraordinary surprise message from Walter Murphy.

Read on.

## Chapter One

# THE RETURN

Black Lightning and Henry had just gone through a gauntlet of an ordeal. Even though one would think that Black Lightning's experiences throughout her space travels could have "toughened" her for her most recent experiences, the fact is that some of the creatures, which she and her associates encountered, were of universal existence in time and space from the beginning of time, albeit in one form or another. The ordeal exhausted them and they needed rest and relaxation.

Elizabeth Sam and Henry Wilson left DESE headquarters hand in hand with stars in their eyes and a warm feeling in their hearts for each other. They were both more than just fond of each other and that presented a problem. Even though Henry matured greatly after his DESE experiences, he still was a high school student. He was not an adult by any means and would have to wait four years to achieve that ripe old age. It was possible that the DESE adventure might have caused the development of premature grey hairs despite his age. However, the traumatic episodes and stresses did not cause the development of even one grey hair.

Henry still had a mother and father. He would have to account to them regarding his activities and he had to live at home. It was fortunate that Mary Kent was able to help him in his activities at DESE by having school officials create special assignments for him in civics classes to which his parents assented. That enabled his absence from home and trips on DESE assignments. Henry's parents were none the wiser.

It bothered Henry that he kept his parents in the dark concerning his special "gifts". He assumed that at some future date all would be revealed to them. However, Henry had no idea about the "how" of such revelation. He would love to relate the stories of his DESE adventures to them, but realized that could never be. He was sworn to secrecy. The most his parents could ever know was that he was enlisted in a special service to his country on a voluntary basis and that such service was honorable but required complete secrecy.

Additionally, revelation to his parents detailing his escapades could put them in danger from forces both known and unknown. That was a risk he was not willing to subject his mother and father. His secret would remain with him, at least for the time being. The less they knew, the safer they would be.

Henry and Elizabeth decided that it was necessary for Henry to maintain the charade of a schoolboy living a "normal" life at home with his parents. Elizabeth would return to Mary Kent's house and continue her life as Black Lightning. After all, she had accustomed herself to a well-developed routine that was now quite a few years old.

Henry and Elizabeth found it difficult to part, but it was a choice thrust upon them by current circumstances. They both mutually agreed on the necessity to keep appearances just as they were before the recent DESE adventure. They expected to meet periodically here and there. However, the fact is that Henry's paper route was still quite viable and that alone would provide for regular meetings at Mary Kent's house.

Black Lightning was not as happy as she was before her DESE experience. She had also changed and had become accustomed to life as a full-fledged human being. Life as a cat in disguise had its restrictions. First of all, it was beneath her station in human terms. After all, she was a gifted Interstellar Starship Yeoman. She had abilities no human could ever conceive. Her diet of salmon and tuna in cans left her instead with a propensity for the more eclectic human diet and lifestyle. Black Lightning, in the form of the charming Elizabeth Sam, developed a liking for feminine clothing styles, especially shoes. Elizabeth spent her life in the form of a cat which is the way the intelligent inhabitants of the planet Ida appeared.

The presence of feet in human form opened a completely new vista for her and the existence of shoes was a delightful and completely new experience. It was an experience that she loved and indulged in their wearing with delight. The continued existence in the form of a cat was a complication in her military station even though her position as a starship officer no longer existed, at least for the moment. She also liked the excitement of interaction with intelligent humans. She enjoyed being human. Black Lightning became a bit unsure of whom she really was, but eventually realized that she could be whomever she wanted to be.

She realized that she could make that change any time she wished.

However, for the moment, her role as Black Lightning, Mary Kent's cat, would be sufficient at least until she has time to digest her situation.

## Chapter Two

# HENRY AND SORCERER MURPHY

Perhaps the meeting was accidental, and perhaps it was not.

Henry's adventures with the D.E.S.E. organization left him quite changed. He was no longer just an ordinary young man, and neither was he an old man. He was somewhere between youth and middle age which is not exactly where his actual numbered age would put him. However, Henry did not display the immaturity and optimism of a carefree, irresponsible, happy-go-lucky youth. He was excessively serious and mature beyond his years. After all, he had met with mythological creatures and even demons. It would be most likely very safe to say that virtually no human being ever meets such beings during their lifetime. Those two experiences alone should be enough to sober anyone into immediate maturity.

Contending with the adventure in meeting such uncommon creatures was not all that Henry had to do. He had also developed an encyclopedic mind. He knew about things he never studied or experienced. He developed the ability to read minds, even unintentionally. He developed the ability to transfer thoughts into the minds of others without their knowing it. He had no idea as to why this was happening to him, of all people. Oddly enough, he was also improving his skills in telekinesis and teleportation. Henry was almost afraid of what skills he would next acquire but he was aware that unknown skills were still developing in his body and in his head. There was no telling where such growth would lead.

It was not enough that he was the son of a Fairfield, Connecticut dentist and a Greenwich, Connecticut schoolteacher mother. He was a young man with extraordinary gifts and abilities.

Those gifts put extra pressure on him. Henry hoped that when he next met his mentor, Jack Henigson, some light might be shed on Henry's uncertainties and further that Jack might provide him with sorely needed reassurances. Jack Henigson had told him earlier that such developments would occur, so the situation was one of which he had to be aware. Jack did not say that as a warning, but perhaps he should have.

Henry knew more than almost anyone around him. Of course, the exceptionally special persons knew more than he did. He defined these people as Jack Henigson, Mr. Xilx, Elizabeth Sam, and Seemore Manlein. He had fearfully taken school exams, but he deliberately entered incorrect answers so that no one could look upon him as some kind of mental freak. Henry liked the idea of just being "ordinary" and he wanted to remain inconspicuous, especially to his friends. He wanted all to be just as it was before he became Jack Henigson's protégé and secret government agents while still a teenager.

The current facts betrayed the truth, however. Henry was no longer just "ordinary" and he never would be again. His dilemma was where and how to fit in. Where to fit in with his friends, his grade level and most importantly, his parents was a worrisome problem with which he struggled on a constant basis. He could not stop his mind from running over all his myriad thoughts. It just kept running on and on, much like the Dragon Roller Coaster at Playland Park in Rye with its slowly rising ups and rapidly descending downs. He could not wait to meet with Jack Henigson on his Thursday collection day. There was much to discuss.

Henry eventually arrived at home and greeted his mother and father. Fortunately, or unfortunately, they were both at home. His parents both rushed to meet their civics-minded son. He was away from home on his supposedly school's civics project for the past week and his parents, mother Cyndy and father missed him and could not wait to hear of Henry's experiences.

Henry already knew what they had in mind because he read their minds even before he entered the house. His quandary was "How could I really tell them what happened? I am sworn to complete secrecy even from my parents. I have to think fast and make something up. Hopefully, it has to be something so boring that they would have no interest in pursuing it further with constant inquiry into details."

Henry mentally intercepted his father's thought that perhaps he met with a senator or a member of the House of Representatives while he was away on his civics class assignments. That was enough of a hint for him to "invent" the tale that his group had met with Senators Lieberman, Shays and Clinton on his civics trip and that he found the meetings very enlightening.

The white lie was not to his liking, but it did satisfy his father who said, "My son, that is terrific! You will be doing great things someday. Mother and I are very, very proud of you."

The praise was delightful, but it induced terrific guilt in Henry's psyche. He made a face when he heard his father's praise. He did not like that feeling at all and swore to himself that he would never tell such a fib to his parents ever again! He knew that his parents would not be able to withstand the shock that their minor son was developing superhuman abilities bordering on the supernatural and a secret government agent to boot!

Henry brought his small suitcase to his room and unpacked it. He did not bring many items with him to DESE headquarters. The government provided essential services and items for him. Mary Kent and her associate, James Barrett, did a remarkable job in supplies as well as accommodation and what-have-you. Henry had minimal essentials to unpack. They included items such as underwear, shirts, socks and several pairs of pants, both semi-formal and leisure types. There were no ties. Henry disliked ties because they reminded him of a hangman's noose and constricted his neck whenever he had to wear one. He felt that ties and "O-rings" were invented by the devil himself. First, the noose around one's neck had to be dangerous. That is why in Old West movies they call it a "Necktie Party". Second, "O-rings" usually go wrong at a critical moment and were usually very hard to repair because they would almost never refit into place properly. Truly, such items could not be of human origin. Unfortunately, Henry suspected the faulty logic as his own emotional problem and not reality.

Henry continued to remove his clothing from his suitcase when something shiny caught his attention. It looked like a dog's license tag and was at the bottom of his suitcase. He knew that he did not place it there and was puzzled at its presence among his clothing. Instead of having the usual identifications embossed on it, this tag was circled in semi-precious stones with what appeared to be an Olympic torch on one side of the medallion.

The torch-like flame on the medallion began to glow as Henry picked it up. Henry looked at the torch side and then paid attention to the obverse. This side contained a bust image of a smiling, mustachioed, sleek looking man. Under the image was inscribed the name of Walter Murphy. Henry stared at the image, which responded to his attention. The image moved, turned its head to look directly at Henry. Murphy's broad smile increased as Henry examined the tag. If that were not enough, the mouth opened and announced the words, "Meet me at the Starbuck's Coffee Shop at the lower end of Greenwich Avenue, across from the movie theatre, at nine PM any evening. I will know whatever day you choose to visit me, but please make it soon."

Henry groaned at seeing a moving, talking image and hearing words coming from what was virtually a type of medallion. He feared and accurately suspected that his life and world would never be the same as it was before DESE and Jack Henigson. Now he knew.

Henry continued to place his clean clothing away and sorted out soiled garments into a separate pile for washing. It did not take very long as he did not take much with him on his way to DESE. Although a respite was in order after the DESE experience, Henry could not easily ignore the existence of a talking, glowing and oversized coin despite his desire to do so. How that coin made its way into his suitcase was a mystery but not surprising when one considers all of Henry's recent DESE associates. Henry knew that he would soon go to the Starbucks meeting place. It was an invitation that his curious side could not ignore. Nonetheless, there was an element of warning and fear about confronting this Walter Murphy, especially alone.

Henry was thinking about the matter when his mother called him down to dinner.

"Henry, come down to dinner. Dad is here and we are waiting for you."

Dinner was excellent. Henry almost forgot that his mother was a near professional chef. Conversation at the dinner table was interesting. Henry caught up on the household events of the past week and mom and dad expressed their joy at having their son back home.

Henry still could read their minds and that annoyed him somewhat. He read that they were still interested in the details of his non-existent senatorial experience. Henry wanted them to relax and simply accept the fact that he was now at home. He found that he could influence their minds to that extent, and he decided that he would slowly inform them of who he now was over a period of months. He would make the induction of such thoughts so that they could acceptably conceive of his "changes" as simply "extraordinary" growth and mental development. He could never have them realize the extent of all his powers and gifts. He would have them marvel and delight in the newly achieved abilities he would reveal to them. His parents would never know that Henry influenced them, and they would believe that such realizations were their own.

Henry recognized this method of revelation as deception and was not fully happy about it. Nevertheless, it was all he could do for the moment and some honesty did exist in having them know about the "gifts" their son had developed, to a limited extent. His parents felt that he was simply tired from his school trip and did not press him for details, at least not immediately.

It was at dinner that Henry kept thinking of the coin's message. He now kept it in his pocket. He felt that he needed to keep it close to himself for some subconscious reason. It was as though he was compelled to keep it in close access. His mind was going a million miles per hour between that coin and influencing his parents' thoughts. He decided that he would make telepathic contact with Elizabeth Sam in the hope that she would accompany him to meet Walter Murphy.

## Chapter Three

# SORCERER MURPHY

It took only a few seconds after the thought originated in Henry's mind that Elizabeth responded.

"Of course, Henry; I am already bored with nothing to do. I would love to meet this "Walter Murphy". Where do you want to meet?" telepathed Elizabeth.

"I am to meet him at the Starbucks Coffee Shop on Greenwich Avenue. It is just diagonally across from the movie theatre." Henry answered.

"That is a great place. It is usually quite busy and a heavy duty hangout for many teenagers, most likely you included!" teased Elizabeth.

"I have spent my share of time there; that is for certain." Henry responded.

"It is not a quiet place. It is very public. We should be all right there. I mean that I do not think there is any danger for us there." Elizabeth answered.

"I see that you sense my worry. I do not know who this person is or how or why he wants to meet with me. He somehow placed a talking coin in my suitcase and it said that I could meet him any evening at Starbucks and that he would know when I would be there to meet him", Henry telepathed back.

"Really", said a now curious Elizabeth. "I wonder if he is one of the "gifted" persons in your group. Jack Henigson might know. Perhaps we should do a telepathic "conference" call and ask him."

"That sounds like a great idea", Henry replied. "Let us do just that right now."

The thought had barely been transmitted to Elizabeth when Jack Henigson's telepathic voice entered the conversation.

"Well, well, well", came the supercilious comment. "The non-stop duo has not yet had enough, have you? Your question as to whether a certain individual is a member of the "Extraordinarily Gifted Intelligentsia Club", to which we belong, is an interesting one indeed", telepathed Jack.

"Why Jack, you were eavesdropping, weren't you? Shame, shame Jack, but you are right. Who is this person anyway?" returned Henry.

"Not at all. We watch out for each other. Since you are still a novice, Mr. Xilx and I have a protective interest in your welfare. We are monitoring you and hoping that you will not get into any trouble with your newfound gifts", thought transferred Jack. "Now tell me who are you interested in learning about?"

"It is not a simple matter. This person's name is Walter Murphy. Somehow, he had a talking coin placed in my suitcase at some point during my DESE experience. It said that I should meet him any evening at the local Starbucks Coffee Shop", answered Henry. "I know nothing about him or what the reason could be to have me meet with him."

"Very interesting", said Jack. "Any evening, you say. How do you think he would know what evening you might pick? Any evening indeed says he! I wonder if he is watching the place or lives nearby or something." Jack was thinking aloud, but mental telepathically.

He continued, "I do not think that I know him either. Let me look into the matter before you meet with him. I want it to be safe for you. I will be in touch shortly. In the meantime, you and Elizabeth are to stay put" Henigson commanded.

## Chapter Four

# HENIGSON'S REPORT

Jack Henigson initiated the telepathic "telephone" contact to Henry and made it a conference call to include Elizabeth and Mr. Xilx.

"Well, Henry", Jack Henigson began, "Mr. Xilx and I have both telepathed around the world regarding this Walter Murphy person. He is well known in certain circles and he has a past."

Even though Henry received Jack's telepathy it was Elizabeth who responded. "Very interesting." She began. "I have never heard of him. He could not be a famous person. What do you mean that he is "well-known" in certain circles? What do you mean by that? What exactly are those so-called circles?"

"Well", continued Jack, "they are the literal circles and other weird shapes one sees from high in the air and from outer space. The so called mysterious "crop circles" which appear overnight and without warning or any other witness to their happening. Those are only one set of "circles" to which Mr. Murphy has been linked. No one knows where they come from, how they are formed and what the reason for their formation is."

"Curious" said both Elizabeth and Henry at the very same instant as in a chorus.

Henry asked, "Is there more?"

"But of course," said an almost pompous Mr. Xilx. "A man like Mr. Murphy is apparently a very complex individual. The fact that he was able to penetrate the secure DESE perimeters to place that "coin" in your suitcase attests to that. He apparently has some very special abilities. We only seem to have scratched the surface of his personal attributes. While he was not part of DESE, it is obvious that he is also one of our "gifted" club types. The real question is whether he is the side of good or not. That is a most likely probability because just about our entire "gifted" group is on the side of good. As a matter of fact, I have never known of anyone of our "club" who was not."

Jack added, "I also have never known of any of the so-called "gifted" ones who were ever on the side of evil. It is most likely that Mr. Murphy is of the "good" sort and is one of "us"."

"I wonder what he wants with me?" puzzled Henry. "Just as long as he is not an agent of the evil witches we just encountered and seeking some kind of revenge or to get even, as it were, I won't be concerned."

"I truly doubt that", added Jack Henigson. "Those witches will not be heard from for quite a while; I'll bet my pipe on that!"

Mr. Xilx laughed approvingly. He was hoping that Jack might lose that bet. He would have liked nothing more than to get that smelly pipe out of the house.

Mr. Xilx then said, "I think you should go and meet this Mr. Murphy and see what this is all about. Take Elizabeth with you and go together. They say there is security in numbers. Jack and I will be keeping an eye on you and be within telepathic earshot. If you should need us, we will show up in an instant."

Jack added, "Hopefully, that will not be necessary."

"Ditto," replied Henry. "I certainly hope not, but Murphy's apparent special abilities still leave the chance of risk open." Henry said a bit concerned. Then he added cheerfully, "Nothing ventured, nothing gained! So goes the saying and I think so will go Elizabeth and Henry as well!"

Elizabeth entered the telepathic "chat room" and added, "Then it is settled. Henry and I will go to the Greenwich Avenue Starbucks to meet Mr. Murphy. The question then is "when?""

Henry said, "That is easy. How about now?"

"All right, now is as good a time as any. I will be at your place in a few seconds, Henry. Then we can walk to Starbucks together." Elizabeth replied.

Jack and Mr. Xilx concurred. "It is late in the afternoon. You will be there just in time for the start of evening as Mr. Murphy asked. It all comes together then, does it not?"

"Right." Henry answered. "It will be as Murphy designated."

There was then a soft, quite feminine "swoosh" and Elizabeth appeared at Henry's side, suitably attired in the young, almost adult, fashion of the day.

"I'm ready Henry. Let's go!" commanded Elizabeth.

# GREENWICH AVENUE STARBUCKS

Customers were milling about, and the place was packed with many of Henry's friends. He was most certainly not alone. That only added to the curiousness of the Mr. Murphy request to meet him at this location. There certainly was nothing private about this location. Mr. Murphy could not have evil intentions against Henry, or he would never have chosen such a public place.

The pair ordered a latte' and managed to find a table out of sheer luck. The very second, they had their latte's in their hands, the table immediately behind them was vacated and they claimed it. They just sat there, staring into each other's eyes. Elizabeth broke the silence between them.

"Well, Henry, when do you suppose that Mr. Murphy will show up?" she asked.

Henry shrugged and said, "I know as much as you do. I have no idea whatsoever."

A more insistent and almost impatient Elizabeth asked, "Well, what did he tell you? What was his message to you? He must have told you something about how he would make contact. Did he not?"

Henry squirmed under the persistent questions and answered, "I don't think so."

Henry looked up to the ceiling, still uneasy, but he was trying hard to recall any information regarding meeting his contact. He paused a second and then raising his index finger he said, "Now I remember. He said that he would know when I was here."

Elizabeth was still not satisfied with that answer. She said, "All right. Where is he?"

A defensive Henry now answered, "I do not know! We have only been here twenty minutes. Cool your heels and let's not complain at least until a half hour passes by!"

Elizabeth was now apologetic. "I am sorry Henry. You are right. I should not be impatient. You have ten more minutes."

They both laughed at her statement. Then they waited and waited. The crowd in the restaurant thinned out as the movie theatres in the area began their showings. This was apparently the pre-movie rendezvous.

One of the personnel behind the counter approached the pair. As he approached, he gave them a big smile and asked, "Aren't you going to see the movie. I heard that it is a fantastic release, and the theatre is just across the street. There is another movie theatre on Railroad Avenue around the corner."

Henry responded, "Not really. We are waiting to meet someone."

The waiter responded, "I know. You are expecting to meet with me. I am Walter Murphy, and I am happy to meet you, Henry, and your friend, Elizabeth, as well."

Henry and Elizabeth were both stunned. Not only were they shocked by the unexpected revelation of Walter Murphy as a Starbucks service person but more so at his displayed knowledge regarding who they were, even the existence of Elizabeth.

Before the two visitors had a chance to respond, Walter Murphy explained, "I know that you are surprised at my knowing who you are. Do not be. I am one of the gifted sort. I am one of you."

A quiet and shocked Elizabeth just sat there, mouth wide open, and stared dumbfounded at Henry. Henry quietly returned the same dumbfounded stare.

## Chapter Six

# INDIGNATION

"**W**hat do you mean by "I am one of you"? How are you one of us anyway? Why did you have us wait so long to have us meet you? We're just sitting here twiddling our thumbs waiting for the mysterious "you" to show up at your own sweet leisure. We've been sitting here almost three quarters of an hour getting bored and getting ready to leave. Frankly, I am ticked!" Elizabeth let her feelings be known in a not too soft and feminine voice.

Walter was taken aback. His eyebrows elevated and he raised his arms in defense. He quickly regained his composure as did Elizabeth, and said, "I sincerely apologize, Elizabeth. I thought it was you but I needed to be certain. One cannot walk up to perfect strangers and say that I am the one they were waiting for. How would that appear if they were not the ones waiting for me? It would only appear as though it were some kind of a "come-on"! Either that or they would think that I was some kind of nut."

"So?" retorted a supercilious Elizabeth.

"I waited until the move crowd dissipated somewhat and then my chances of knowing where Henry was would be improved. Also, the fewer people in the crowd, the more "private" our meeting would be", explained a more confident Mr. Murphy with great satisfaction.

"Why the subterfuge if you are "one of us"? Why was that necessary? Why did you not just reach out men-telepathically, a word I just invented, and communicate that way?", Elizabeth continued.

"That is easily explained, Elizabeth" Walter replied. "The way I learned who you are is the problem. Should I have contacted you "men-telepathically", as you say, my communication to either of you might be intercepted. You do know that although most of "us" have good thoughts and know right from wrong, there are always those who may not share our ideals."

Henry and Elizabeth, now more relaxed after Walter Murphy's appearance out of the realm of mystery, were now fully attentive to Murphy's words.

Walter went on, "You and I both know that there are also those who can communicate "men-telepathically" and who are not "one of us". For example, your Mr. Xilx and Seemore Manlein as well as you, Elizabeth."

Henry and Elizabeth were both shocked at that statement. After all, Elizabeth, Mr. Xilx and Seemore were extremely helpful in defeating the evil witches and their demonic allies.

Continuing, Walter added, "I know that you are shocked by that statement, but it goes to demonstrate the fact that others can intercept our thought transfers, even all around the world."

Walter apologetically added, "I do not mean to offend you, Elizabeth, since I know that only goodness lies within you and the others. I only use that as an example to illustrate that it can be quite easy to intercept an unguarded thought transmission."

Elizabeth and Henry both acknowledged the truth about which Walter was speaking. They continued giving him their full attention.

"I also use that as an illustration that others, who are not of our "sort", and some of whom may not even be of our world, can also receive mental telepathic thought and communication. Thus, such communication may not be private at all!" Walter now paused to catch his breath. His explanations were coming a high speed and he needed the moment.

That moment allowed Henry to ask "All that is very understandable and very interesting, but what is the reason for your contacting me by a talking medallion?

Walter replied, "That is easy to explain. The medallion is secure. Communication that way is not intercepted. It is simple and direct. and only between you, Henry, and I.

Henry and Elizabeth turned their heads towards each other at the very same moment and their looks alone attested to the validity of Murphy's statement. Neither Henry nor Elizabeth was efficient into "cloaking" their mental messages. Murphy was right and there could be no argument there.

Regaining their composure, both Henry and Elizabeth asked simultaneously in one voice, "So what is this "secret". What it this "mystery" all about anyway?"

"Henry", continued Murphy, "I am part of the section of "Intelligentsia" which is called the CIA. No, not the well-known CIA but the CIA I belong to is the "Cognitive Intelligentsia Agency". We keep it a bit more secretive and more private. We are an agency which concerns itself with the doings of "gifted" individuals such as yourself."

Henry's curiosity peaked. "Why would anyone ever be interested in what I, or others like me, would be doing? You need to explain, please."

Murphy continued, "Henry, not all gifted individuals are as altruistic as you and your friends. Unfortunately, there are those among us who do not have unselfish goals but use their gifts to help themselves to that which is not theirs. They have either no or only minimal interest in helping their fellow man and the environment for the better. In short, they are dishonest and hurt not only innocent persons but also their surroundings. The destroy hope and dreams for some people and they are only interested in their own selfish goals."

"What does that have to do with me?" Henry asked.

"Henry, as a recruit in the "Intelligentsia", you are in danger" explained a cryptic and mysterious Walter Murphy with eyebrows cocked, eyes wide opened as well as a wry expression on his mouth as he made this point.

"What? I never joined any agency!" Henry, now becoming a bit upset with this news as well its mystery asked, "In danger of what?"

"Henry, you are in danger of being remotely controlled and influenced. I know because that is what they did to me!" Walter exclaimed.

"Nonsense! No one can control me. I am my own person and I control myself.

"Henry", Murphy continued, "This world is a mixture of opposites. There is "plus" and there is "minus". There is "ying" and there is "yang". There is "good" and there is "bad". There are those who hate and those who love. There is vengeance and there is forgiveness."

"So?" asked a skeptical Henry. "What does that have to do with me?"

"A lot." Murphy answered. "A lot indeed. There are those who see your gifts as a means to wealth and to obtain those material things in life which they do not have to work for. Those material things are unearned. That means those who seek them do not really deserve them. They have not earned the right to own them. In short, these individuals are thieves and what they thus possess are stolen items of varying sorts."

"I understand what you are saying", said Henry. "But once more, what does that have to do with me?"

Murphy replied, "Henry, can you not see? Your abilities and newly found infantile gifts are powers that can help these thieves achieve their goals. Should criminal elements learn how to manipulate your abilities by "remote control" they can achieve their ends at your expense. What is worse, they may be able to do so without you even being aware of your actions."

"I cannot believe that. That is not possible", Henry exclaimed. Henry and Elizabeth both expressed incredulity at that last statement.

Murphy continued, "I am not toying with you. It is a fact. I know because I was victimized in the past. Fortunately, I was able to escape by sheer dumb luck."

"Henry, the world is full of those who steal, cheat and hurt others, sometimes not only because of greed but also because they are evil and simply enjoy hurting others. They use devices of all kinds to achieve their ends." Walter paused and awaited Henry's reaction. Henry just sat there with his mouth open but speechless.

Walter continued, "Henry, there exist spectacles, which can be placed on a book or on a shelf which permit its owner or other possessor to "see" the events happening before it, just as if that owner were actually wearing them, although he is not. Distance makes no difference, no matter how far. That owner, a spy, can be hundreds of miles away. These are enchanted spectacles. Eyeballs sometimes appear in those spyglasses for a fast moment or two, looking right, left, up and down, searching and searching in all directions, although they are attached to nobody.

Who knows how many exist, where they came from or whoever made them. I am certain that they are still being made."

"Henry, you may see a person wearing glasses. That person may not know that although he can use those spectacles to see what is before him but that whatever he sees is also being seen by another, but alien, foreign party who was not invited to the viewing. These are charmed spectacles, which see without being worn or even in the immediate possession of its "other" owner.

This is the nature of your new world, Henry. Beware if you find a pair of glasses which you may think someone has lost. Keep them folded and in a case so that you can be certain that they cannot "see" out. Once they are unfolded, their transmission capabilities are activated. They may be enchanted spying spectacles, but one cannot know for certain. It is better to be safe than sorry, as the saying goes."

"That is not all, Henry. One must also beware of what one wears on one's head as well. This is the most insidious of all devices. A person's favorite hat is another enchanted spying device. Worse than just spying, a hat of this type can be made to control another's thoughts as well. We all know that DESE has devices which can change people's minds. However, this item, the enchanted hat, is not a DESE device. Once it is placed on a duped party's head, his thoughts are transmitted to his enemy. Furthermore, that enemy can use the "hat" device to induce his own thoughts, desires and goals into the victim's mind, thus making him think that such thoughts are his own."

A now very excited Walter Murphy became quite animated and continued speaking to the silent and awestruck couple before him. "Henry, there are shoes, which may become your favorite pair, but they cannot be yours. They belong to an enemy, unknown to you, who may have presented them to you as a gift. Perhaps they were a pair in a store where the pair of shoes were placed with a charm placed upon them with the purpose of attracting you, Henry. Those shoes could be made to specifically attract you just as certainly as a Cupid's arrow might be aimed at you. Such could be the design, but the intent could be evil." "Henry, those shoes, once placed on your feet would have incredible power. The power would be to perform the commanded deed of its master whether for good or not. You would not even be aware that such shoes have led you where you would not go in your good sense."

Henry looked not only doubtful, but also perturbed. He looked Walter directly in the eyes and said, "Such a thing is not possible. Shoes and eyeglasses!" Henry exclaimed in disdain. "Sheer nonsense!"

Walter just stood there, returning Henry's direct eye in the eye stare, and was silent, but only momentarily. "Henry, that is not all. Should you wear a favorite cap or other type of hat the results could be even worse. If the same enemy made that cap or hat, not only would your current thoughts become known by that individual, but he could also place different thoughts into your mind. These are enchanted spying and mind controlling devices which even DESE is not aware."

The insistent earnest speech coming from Walter was beginning to influence Henry. He was starting to question himself. His initial reaction was starting to change. Ever since his DESE experiences, Henry realized that anything was possible, including every word that Walter Murphy uttered.

Henry wondered as Murphy was speaking, "How did this man, who essentially came out of nowhere, even know about him? How did he know that Henry was new to the world of mystery, magic, and wonderment? Henry guessed that his mind was essentially an open book for any "gifted" person to inspect. After all, Jack Henigson and Mr. Xilx told him that he needed greater education in his abilities to mask his thoughts. Henry knew that he needed improvement. That was an indisputable fact. After all, he was only thinking about contacting Elizabeth when she called him out of the blue. She told him that she had read his thoughts and thus her sudden telephone call.

Henry surmised that such had to be the only way Walter could have known all the details of Henry's existence and his state of inexperience in the world of magic as well as other magical things and wonderments. Henry's thoughts had to leak out into the world like a sieve! He was beginning to realize that he might really be subject to anyone's intervention or worse.

Henry's mindset changed and reoriented itself to consider all that Walter had to relate to him. He went from a "no way!" mindset to "it could be true" way of thinking.

Henry would quiet himself and pay attention to Walter's words. Henry also was very interested in where all Walter's words and divulgence of information from Walter was heading. Why would Walter even bother either to contact Henry or even to warn him that he was in danger? Why indeed!

Elizabeth gave Henry a knowing and understanding glance.

That was not really needed as she had already read his thoughts. As a matter of fact, so did Walter Murphy. Henry was an open book and no thoughts of his were private. Elizabeth sat quietly during Walter Murphy's lecture.

She always knew Henry's thoughts and she had to agree with Walter although began to realize that Henry might be in dangerous territory. She had to recognize that possibility now. It could not be disputed. After all, she immediately knew Henry's thoughts as they were born in his head! Surely, those who were interested and able to "tune in" to Henry's thoughts could easily do so. The rest of the world might know his thoughts too! That was neither safe nor wise. She realized that Murphy's statements rang true. Henry certainly was in danger. He was young and very inexperienced regarding his gifts and magical abilities. He was naïve, trusting and truly an easy mark for anyone who had the ability to take advantage of him. Such an individual must be either a "gifted one" or a totally wicked and malevolent individual, or group, with special powers. He was truly and easy mark for anyone who had the ability to take advantage of him. He was truly and easy mark for anyone who had the ability to take advantage of him

The pair's resistance and reluctance to trust Murphy changed. Now they really felt a sincere and urgent need to know more. Indeed, they _had_ to know more. They had to know all that there was to know. Murphy was their unelected, uninvited voluntary source. Whatever he had in the way of information was everything that Elizabeth and Henry had to learn and learn it quickly for their own mutual safety.

"Henry, these evil people just want to use you and your special abilities to meet their goals, whatever they might be. They do not care a "twit" about you as a person or even as a human being. Henry, you must realize that such persons are "sneaks" and being so, they are most certainly not honest. They just want to use you, Henry. Just use you!" Murphy just suddenly stopped talking and waited for Henry's response.

"Ye Gads!" shouted Henry using an immediate but quite antiquated exclamation and gesturing with his arms. "Why are you telling me this?

Why should you care? What interest is it to you? What, exactly, do you have in mind?" asked a quizzical Henry.

Henry's question was anticipated by all at the table, and via telepathy, so was Mr. Xilx and Jack Henigson attentive to Walter's reply.

## Chapter Seven

# INTERNATIONAL INTRIGUE

While Henry and Elizabeth were being educated by Walter at Starbucks, Jack Henigson was busy doing international research regarding Walter Murphy. Jack could still listen in on the Greenwich Avenue conversation, but he kept it in the background of his mind. The more conscious elements of his telepathic mind were turning the mental pages of his friends and fellow agents and "gifted" acquaintances around the world. He was investigating Walter Murphy to the "$N^{th}$" degree. When Jack was finished investigating, he would know all that ever was recorded regarding the mysterious Walter Murphy. No stone would be left unturned, and no record or book could have its pages delved through more quickly. Jack was on the run. He would not permit anything to hurt Henry or Jack's other friends.

He learned that Walter Murphy became involved with Interpol about twenty years earlier when he was just a youth, which would have put him at about Henry's age. It was not a joyous occasion for Walter because he became embroiled in an international debacle concerning Information Technology Crime.

So-called "working parties" were developed under the guidance of the Interpol General Secretariat and, in Walter's case and some others, the investigating members were the experienced heads of national computer crime units. Each was from different parts of the world and from different cultures. They all were members of the Information Technology Crime unit, the ITC, for short.

They would meet three times a year dealing with major international criminal matters and revise their Information Technology Crime Investigation Manual, a compiled Computer Crime Manual, which is a more precise label, and now available on CD. That is in keeping with the times.

It turned out that Walter was not on the side of the law at all. He was involved in stealing monies and valuables such as gems and gold from various sources around the world but ironically not for his own benefit. All his thefts were to create wealth.

Unfortunately for Walter, that wealth was something he never saw. The thefts were something he never knew he committed. His body was his, but not under his control, and for that matter, neither was his mind. Walter was more of a remote-controlled robot with all the attributes a person of the "gifted" sort could muster. Continuing the unfortunate, even those "gifts" were not in his conscious control, but rather under the influence of others, some great distance away.

The lack of being under his own powers was not constant. Most of the time he was his own man. There were only periodic situations and circumstances that he would be under the control of others, namely Cameron Schultz.

## Chapter Eight

# BEHIND THE SCENE

**W**hile Henry and Walter were busily discussing possible future and current events, a very distant location was busy developing the prospect of a new adventure for Henry.

Cameron Schultz was concentrating intensely on the wall mirror before him. He was very attentive. The room was quiet, and one could almost hear floating dust particles in the air. That was as silent as anything! There is no greater silence, even in a tomb. As Cameron concentrated, he gently closed his eyes, but furrows developed on his forehead as concentration intensified. Another frame projected itself about three feet from the mirror and stood shimmering before him. It was then that Cameron opened his eyes and as he did so the furrowed brow faded. Cameron stared into the projection.

Cameron was doing more than just looking though. He was also listening! Silence was extremely necessary. Cameron had tuned into the Henry-Walter telepathic "station" with great interest. He was able actually to "see" wavy images of Henry and Walter at the Greenwich Avenue Starbucks in the water before him, but it was quite a bit more difficult to "hear". Cameron had used this "bowl of water" technique before to his great advantage.

Cameron is the leader of an international information and technology theft ring. Cameron had the advantage of the same special "talents" Henry was in the middle of developing. Walter's talents exceeded those which even Jack Henigson possessed. Cameron was at least on a par with Walter's abilities. The only exception is that Cameron's goals were not honorable but criminal. Cameron was the individual who took advantage of Walter while in his early and vulnerable developmental stage.

This is what Walter wished to keep Henry from experiencing. It would be an additional triumph for Walter if he should also be able to "even the score" with the malevolent individuals that put him through his earlier "hell".

Unknown, even to Cameron, was the fact that Interpol, the international crime fighting organization, found Cameron to be a "person of interest" regarding international crimes including the theft of Crown Jewels belonging to the English queen despite being well-secured inside the Tower of London. However, not all the Crown Jewels were stolen, only bits and pieces, several rubies here, some diamonds there and multiple emeralds for good measure. No extraordinarily large gems were taken but only those items which were not conspicuously obvious, but items which would eventually be noticed.

How the items were removed remains a mystery to this day. The doors and security remained firm. No detection, electronic, laser beams or cameras, were ever alerted. No alarms were sounded, and no humans or animals were ever detected or seen within the secured areas. The crime did take place and the question remains, how? Equally mysterious is who perpetrated the act?

Scotland Yard never did recover the gems, worth several million pounds, but they learned that Cameron Schulz was visiting England at the time. They were alerted to Cameron's existence in England by Interpol prior to his arrival. He never was convicted of a crime anywhere and they had no reason to deny him entry.

Cameron made the Interpol list of Suspicious Persons only because of his constant proximity to areas where similar crimes had occurred. The crimes were always mysteriously performed and always without clues. The only common element was Cameron Schulz's proximity to the crime scene.

It was this constancy of Cameron's nearness to several crime scenes that Scotland Yard did keep a very close tab on Cameron during his English visit. All they ever noticed was that Cameron took in all the usual touristy sights, including the Tower of London, the nearby church where hundreds of people had been buried, and of course, the precious gems, crown and scepter display, all in the same area.

Cameron came in, went through, along with many others, looking at and being amazed by the different objects sealed behind the glass enclosure. To make the situation even more mysterious, two Secret Agents entered the exposition site, one before Cameron and one behind him. They did not miss a thing. Cameron was no different than anyone else. He was supposedly just a "normal" tourist and nothing more.

Scotland Yard is well trained in the apprehension of criminals. However, the continuing mystery of precious gems disappearing from inside the Tower of London is quite perturbing to the powers that be. What is most puzzling is that after the thieves made access to the gems was the fact that these thieves were able to remove only select gems by virtually "dissecting" the Scepter and Crown and taking only some of the gems. It appears the event of theft was more a taunt rather than a theft.

Of course, the value of the items stolen makes the event a theft and not just a tease. Violation of very high security without complete thievery makes it a tease. Cameron's continuing presence in the vicinity of such happenings makes it more of a mystery.

Interpol has actively been involved for several years in combating Information Technology Crime. Rather than 're-inventing the wheel', the Interpol General Secretariat harnessed the expertise of its members in the field of Information Technology Crime (ITC) via a 'working party' or a group of expert's organization. In this instance, the working party consists of the heads or experienced members of national and international computer crime units. These working parties are designed to reflect regional expertise and exist in Europe, Asia, and the Americas and in Africa. All working parties are in different stages of development.

Cameron's inability to control his very private personal being was not constant. Most of the time, he was his own man. There were only periodic situations and circumstances that he would be under the control of others, namely Cameron. Fortunately, those times were few and far between. However, they were frequent enough that Walter sensed that something was not quite right. He had found that there were "gaps" in his daily, and sometimes weekly, routine. Walter sometimes found himself in distant parts of the world and did not know how he arrived there. He sometimes found that he had items in his possession that were not his. He could tell that they were either items of great importance or value. He was puzzled as to how such materials came to be in his possession!

Walter was increasingly surprised when he read in the papers that the items he now possessed were stolen. Radio and television news would be rattling on about how secret corporate, or government papers were mysteriously "missing" or that precious gems, gold and platinum was also gone from its safe-keeping vaults from different places around the world. The latter was considered a greater mystery because of the weight and mass of the precious metals.

On all occasions, there were no witnesses. No one saw anything come or go. The loss of such precious items was truly mysterious. Insurance companies would classify the loss as a "mysterious" disappearance. The puzzle was compounded when Walter found that he possessed some of the items described in the news releases. Walter became very much alarmed. He had no idea how they came to be in his possession, but he knew something was wrong. This happened more than once and, as a result, Walter was now alerted. He also knew that these stolen items had to be returned. He was not certain as to how to do that.

He first asked himself from where the booty came. Walter developed the additional ability to place his mind into a meditative trance. He would visualize his past. It was like running a movie film backwards. "Yes", he would say to himself, "that was where I was and that was what I did. But before that…"

Walter would continue his trance stupor to go back in time, moment-by-moment and day-by-day. He became so adept at this technique that he was able to go back in time, minute-by-minute, for more than a year. It was through this unique ability that he was able to discover that he was being controlled by a foreign entity.

Walter never learned who that individual was, but he did learn to "cloak" his thoughts and his mind; he thus became able to create a "protective" shield over his being, his thoughts and mental communications with others.

Henry did not have this protective ability yet. His mind, his thoughts, communications and daily routine were an open book. Those who were "gifted", but did not share the malevolent intentions of Cameron Schultz, could "tune in" to the "Henry" broadcasts and party line- like conversations. Most were not interested.

Walter thus learned about Henry by "tuning in" to his uncloaked thoughts and communications with others. Walter saw his younger defenseless self in Henry and recognized his super abilities and gifts. He became a benevolent being because of his own history. He learned more of Henry than Henry knew of himself. "Here," said Walter to himself "is a unique and super gifted individual that reminds me of myself many innocent years ago." Walter became determined to protect Henry from the likes of Cameron Schulz. Walter thus determined that he would become Henry's mentor, guide and protector. Walter recognized that this task would be difficult because Henry did not know him. It would likely be difficult to gain Henry's trust.

## Chapter Nine

# CAMERON SCHULTZ

When Cameron was but a boy of twelve, he was orphaned. His mother and father were both lost in an unexplained train accident in Spain. Terrorism was suspected. He had no siblings. Cameron had only one aunt who became his surrogate mother. She was destitute and had a very difficult time keeping house and hearth together. Nevertheless, she made a valiant effort to do both, and she succeeded.

Cameron did his share. He helped at home and after he turned sixteen, he worked hard and helped provide additional family income.

It was not easy for Cameron or his Aunt Matilda. Aunt Matilda was a very intelligent woman, although neither a scholar nor a professional. She had all the major secretarial capabilities, each of which she was exceedingly excellent. Typing, shorthand, accounting et cetera were all in her forte'.

Unfortunately, she was never able to make a good living at secretarial employment and she found it necessary to supplement her income by working one day each weekend cleaning houses and doing outside laundry.

Cameron worked at the local meat packing company part time and at the local magic shop. He did all this while maintaining excellent grades in school. He was at the top of his class and even skipped a grade because of his learning abilities.

His greatest interests were science, math, history and English. He exceeded expectations in all subjects, and it was determined that Cameron was at "genius" level.

His work at the meat packing plant was unremarkable. However, his work at the magic shop, his second job, spurred his curiosity. It was here that Cameron's interests developed into something more than dealing with just simple magic tricks.

Cameron found that while a magic trick was to achieve a certain result, he could make that result change at will. If a two-headed coin were flipped, there was no choice but that one of the heads would turn up in a person's palm. Cameron was able to change that.

For instance, the two-headed coin was flipped. The observer would expect one head to show up as there is no "tail" opposite side. Cameron was able to make that coin show a supposedly "non-existent tail" instead. This was to the surprise of Cameron, the observer, and the shop owner. The magic shop owner was more than just amazed. He was shocked and not happy. The trick was to work as designed. How could he sell a trick that did not work as advertised? The shop owner was puzzled and curious and became wary and suspicious of Cameron. He wondered how this young person performed the trick.

The double headed coin would not show the "tail" side of the coin for long. It would revert to the "head" side after a few minutes. If one were observing, the change would happen before their eyes. That made the "trick" even more curious.

That curiosity was not the shop owners' alone. Cameron was as surprised as anyone else! He did not know how the unexpected happened. He only thought that it would be curious if a "tail" showed up and then it did!

Cameron was also concerned with how that happened as well. He did not put any great effort into creating the change. He only thought, "Would it not be extraordinary if the tail of that coin showed up." The thought ran through his mind again and again.

The shop owner thereafter viewed Cameron with both awe and respect. "This is no ordinary boy", he thought to himself.

Cameron put aside the occurrence for the moment and put the thought out of his mind. He had the day's chores and duties to perform. He would mentally revisit the event later. Similar events followed the dull existence of a hard-working Cameron. He recognized that he had influence over matters to the point of transmutation from one form to another. He learned that he had a mental "tick" or a "switch" in his head that permitted him to turn his virtual "supernatural" ability on and off at will. He worked on developing this ability for several months.

He would stare at a stoplight and would be able to make it change from red to yellow to green. He could make the arrow turn signal change at will as well. Automobile drivers waiting in traffic for the light to change in their favor were very unhappy as Cameron changed from one signal color to another within a few seconds of each other. They did not know what to make of the confusion, and after a while, they tended to ignore the senseless signal changes, and took chances with oncoming traffic. There were some accidents. Walter was not intentionally causing the light signal changes and he only became aware of the situation when he was a passenger in a taxicab harassed by the errant signal light.

This was a good thing, in a way, because when he realized that he was causing the light changing, he was able to begin to control the effect of his thoughts and the actions they caused in his environment as well. This was also a good thing, because Cameron just discovered that he had this new ability, which was hard for him to fathom. In time, he was able to control this novel power and use it as needed. His thoughts now were no longer "random" but purposeful instead.

Chapter Ten

# WARY TRUST

**M**uch was going on in Henry's world, mind and heart. He was still able to develop a small grasp of the significant changes he was going through and the new developments in his being. He almost imperceptibly became more and more aware of Cameron Shultz's presence in his head. Slowly his awareness of this now unwelcome foreign cerebral invasion became complete. He now was able successfully to repel any commands from Shultz but made a permanent note of everything Shultz telepathed to him for reference's sake.

He recalled his sessions with Walter Murphy beginning with the Starbucks encounter. He began to understand where Walter was coming from, although he did not trust him as his entry into his life was suspect. Walter entered without invitation or any mutual introduction. He came in out of the blue. He came from nowhere at all, except the ethereal miasma of Henry's uncontrolled and unfettered intellectual brain wave emissions into the void of space. Henry's mind was fair game at least up to now.

Henry began to realize the reality of Walter's warnings. He was serious and earnest. Cameron Shultz's commands to Henry were not honorable ones. They led to theft and other types of petty crime. Henry realized that Walter had been similarly used but successfully fought back and beat whoever was trying to influence him.

Henry decided that he needed help, not just any help. He realized that he needed especially experienced help. He determined that he would seek out Walter Murphy's counsel. Henry found a new respect for what Walter was trying to accomplish. Walter apparently was honest in his quest to protect Henry from the evil influences of the outside world, especially from people like Cameron Shultz.

Henry really developed selectivity in sending out his thoughts. He developed sort of a "setting" as to where he would not fully protect emanating thought wave reception. Those whom he trusted the most were within his "circle" of allies and friends. He did not create a barrier against them. He felt that should he ever be in trouble or had endangering thoughts, that his closest friends could "pop up" and enter his thought process and he would be able to have a mental consultation and counsel with them. This is his defensive perimeter.

"Henry!" came the loud exclamation. It's sudden loudness in his head startled and jolted him upright and he immediately became alert and "online" with Elizabeth. He was shocked out of his mental exercise of thinking about Walter Murphy and Cameron Shultz to the point of full alertness. He was like a soldier coming to full attention before a shouting drill sergeant.

"Elizabeth!" he exclaimed back (mentally of course), "Please don't ever do that again. If this were a connection by sound you would have destroyed my ear drums. You shocked the begeezus out of me!" said a shaken Henry trying to remain as calm and unshaken as possible.

Henry was very happy when Elizabeth entered his thoughts. "What in the world, or universe in this case, are you planning to do Henry?", she virtually barked at him. Henry jumped. While he always welcomed Elizabeth's counsel, he was not prepared for the sudden and loud entry into his head.

"Elizabeth", he started, "I have been mulling over this problem I have. I don't believe that you know about it." He added hesitantly, "At least that is what I think. I do not know. I do not know what thought of mine may have reached you. I think that I must meet with Walter Murphy and seek his advice with this problem."

Henry went on to explain to Elizabeth how Cameron Shultz had been trying to control him, both his mind and his body, and his conscious and unconscious mind and even when he thought he was asleep. Henry became more aware of the seriousness of his problem as he was explaining the details to Elizabeth. It became obvious to Elizabeth that Henry was very upset and disturbed over this unexpected problem and attack on his person.

"Henry, I understand all that you are explaining. It seems to me that this problem may be bigger than you think. You are inexperienced in this realm of the extraordinary. I am just as inexperienced as you….well maybe that is not one hundred percent true" said a hesitant Elizabeth. But it is true here on earth." Elizabeth offered.

"Yes, go on Elizabeth. Help me more if you can." Transmitted a calmer Henry.

"Yes, well I think we should consult and get advice from Jack Henigson as well. He seems to have a lot of experience in such matters and in the world of the so-called "gifted sort", Elizabeth counseled.

"I agree", replied Henry without hesitation. He had been thinking of doing exactly that but put the ultimate decision to do so on a back burner. He preferred to ignore the matter if he could and put it out of his mind. However, continued pressure from Cameron and the additional supporting "push" from Elizabeth finalized his decision. He would do so and welcomed the help from his old friends.

No sooner than the decision was made, he heard in his head, "Welcome back, Henry. I was wondering when I would hear from you. It has been a while since we last made a connection! "Jack Henigson said cheerfully.

"Jack!" exclaimed Henry. "Welcome. It is good to "hear" your voice again. "I have a problem.""

"I know", Jack responded. "I have been "tuning in" and I have gathered bits and pieces of what you are going through. It is not easy, is it Henry? Not easy at all."

"True", concurred a more sedate Henry. The gathering of old allies tended to make him feel more secure. He was now feeling "protected". It was like being at home. He recalled the coziness and warmth he felt when he fell asleep in the womb of the deep armchair at Jack's house that afternoon in what now seems like a very distant past. The company of reliable friends was nothing to sneeze at. Henry was now willing to take all the help he could get.

## Chapter Eleven

# REUNION OF ALLIES

The threesome continued to converse and, while they talked of old times and their earlier adventures, they each kept the current problem in the back of their minds. This was a curious feat because while it was in the back of their minds, it was contrarily always omnipresent and hanging over their collective heads as well. None of them could admit the seriousness of the problem to themselves.

After all, it was one of "their sort" that was engaging in lawlessness, thievery, and malevolent actions in the most cowardly of manners. He was using the mind and body of one of their own. It is more than despicable; it is betrayal of a "gifted" trust. Each of the "gifted" gains a sense of decency and honesty along with their extraordinary trait. It is an "understood" law between them all.

None of the "gifted" needed to resort to stealing, lying or cheating. Their gifts alone provide all their needs magically and virtually without any effort to achieve. Thought alone produces manifestation of their needs. Therefore, it is a treasonous act to betray those gifts for anything on earth. Whatever a "gifted" individual ever wants is simply "wished" for and there it will be, according to any arrangement they want.

Cameron is not only betraying his "gifts" but he is hurting one of his own. That is deemed extremely bad, but even worse, he is hurting the more "normal" humans he has an obligation to protect as well. This combination demands correction which must come from the "Council of Gift". Each of the gifted knows the other, simply because of proximal mental transmission.

If each wishes, he can know where each of the others are, what they are doing, what they are thinking, if they are in danger and so forth. The gifted have lost their privacy to a large degree between themselves, unless they learn how to "cloak" their giftedness. In a way they are part of a web, somewhat like a spider's. When one part of the web is disturbed, vibrations transmit along the network to all parts of that web.

Fortunately, that web is not universal. It encompasses a circle of friends or allies. There are many such separate webs in the world, and even in the universe. The separate webs do not usually communicate with each other, except in great emergencies. Then it is mostly telepathic and from one member of a web to a member of a separate and distinctly different web.

It was not long before Mr. Xilx entered the "conversation". He did the equivalent of a vocal shout mentally transmitted, "One moment there, my friends, this problem will not be resolved without my help. You need me too. We need each other."

Elizabeth, feeling a need to maintain communication with her Starship Admiral agreed sheepishly, "Of course we need you. We most certainly need to attack this thing together as unit."

Henry added, "But how? We have no idea where this thought, mind and body controlling individual is.

Jack Henigson interjected, "I have a line on Mr. 'Who-ever-he-is'. I did get info on our friend at Starbuck's, did I not?"

Jack waited for agreement and hoped for but never received applause.

Henry said, "That is true, Jack. Thank you. I appreciate what you did do. Do you think that we might be able the find the source of this problem? Jack answered, "Without a doubt. I think that we should find Mr. Walter Murphy. He will be our first source of information. Remember, he is the one who first contacted Henry and intended to protect him. It appears he most certainly has some experience in the matter. I recall he said that he had been similarly taken advantage of. Perhaps he has some powers of which we are not fully aware. Who knows, we may even learn from him as well."

Elizabeth added, "Perhaps we wrote him off too soon. We need to have him meet with us."

## Chapter Twelve

# GRAND ENTRANCE

No sooner had Elizabeth's thoughts sped through the air did they all hear, "Agreed! I knew that in time you all would come around to recognizing that you needed me!", intruded Walter Murphy in loud and obvious delight.

"Let me introduce myself to, as I understand it, Mr. Xilx, Jack Henigson, Elizabeth, and Henry are all part of this "round table". I am Walter Murphy. While I am not really known to you all, I want you to know that I will do my utmost to help," Walter ebulliently volunteered.

Continuing, Walter said, "I would like to meet with all of you and get to know each one of you personally as soon as we can arrange it. Can anyone suggest a good place to meet where we can have some privacy?"

Jack Henigson volunteered. "We can all meet at my place. Since it is my home, it will be as private as needed. Would that be all right with everyone?"

All telepathic voices answered in unison a resounding "Yes!"

It is settled. The next question is "when".

All answered again in unison, "Anytime."

"Well then," Jack answered, "how about right now?"

All in unison they again responded, "Right now is all right," and "Yes".

It is settled.

Seconds later, Elizabeth appeared at Henry's location and had him join her via her communication "rubber band" necklace and together they transported to Jack Henigson's living room. Mr. Xilx was already there since he lived with Jack.

They all waited for the expected arrival of Walter Murphy.

Suddenly, there was a bolt of lightning, and a red, yellow and white colored cloud grew in the middle of Jack's living room. A Roman chariot appeared without horses. Comfortably lounging thereon was Walter Murphy. He de-charioted and stepped down. The chariot, cloud and any traveling debris vanished in a "poof" the moment Walter's foot hit the floor.

"Sorry about the lightning," said Walter. "I no longer use horses because they get excited and sometimes poop upon arrival. It makes a mess. This is neater."

The spectators surrounding the arrival area hesitantly came closer to Walter, none was exactly certain as to what Walter might do next. Eventually they shook Walter's hand and any fear regarding Walter soon eased.

Walter was just as he was at the Greenwich Avenue Starbucks, minus a worker's outfit. Elizabeth and Henry gave him immediate recognition that was mutual. Walter acknowledged their greeting and shook hands. Mr. Xilx saw Walter as appearing to be a genuine, down-to-earth human and smiling, they shook hands. Jack Henigson joined in the protocol of greeting Walter. Jack, however, was a bit more reserved than Mr. Xilx was.

Walter said, "Mr. Xilx, I presume, it is very nice to meet you. I know that there is more to you than meets the eye!"

Mr. Xilx nodded and said, "One should not be surprised that what one sees is not all there is indeed! One can be deceived by appearances; however, I think you are aware of what is behind what is immediately apparent."

Both Mr. Xilx and Walter gave a hearty, although short laugh at Xilx's comment. Walter added a sagacious wink as well. It was apparent that Walter knew more about Mr. Xilx and his history than he was letting on.

Walter added, "We should have a talk. I feel that you have much to teach all of us as well."

Mr. Xilx acknowledged the invitation and answered, "I would be delighted to do so, and I agree."

Each of the attendees took different positions about Jack's living room and prepared for what they hoped would be a very interesting encounter with Walter.

Henry comforted himself in the big armchair and Elizabeth sat next to him in a much less luxurious chair. Mr. Xilx and Jack sat in similar chairs all of which circled and faced Walter Murphy.

## CHAPTER THIRTEEN

# GROUP MEETING: WALTER DEPOSES AND SAYS

"Res Ipso Loquitor," started Walter. Each of the attendees looked at each other in confusion. What in the world was this man saying? They waited for what followed. "The thing speaks for itself," added Walter. It is a legal term in Latin. That is what we are all about and that concerns this meeting.

Jack edged forward almost impatiently and asked, "Very good." He continued almost sarcastically. "Go ahead and tell us. We are all eager to understand what prompted you to contact Henry and raise all this fuss about whatever!"

Walter, calmly and sagaciously spoke gently, and in an almost scholarly teaching voice, "You are all in danger." Walter paused and looked in turn into the eyes of each person.

As he did so, each person shrunk back into their original position with Walter getting the full attention he needed.

Walter quickly related his experiences of being unwittingly controlled, both in mind and body, by a foreign, and perhaps even an alien, force. He told of how a malevolent "gifted", unknown individual had him carry out illegal services for him, but all without Walter being aware that he ever performed the deed. He told them that he assumed it was one of our "sort", but he could not be certain of that. He told them that other influences beyond just the "gifted" might exist and that he felt that he should not simply limit his guesses to the familiar, but to leave an open mind to all possibilities.

"My fellow mental telepaths, we may *all* be in trouble. We can *all* be controlled by external and even foreign forces, which usually are not benevolent, but ranging from criminal to evil in their intentions. This is most true regarding young, inexperienced and gifted individuals, who are innocently unaware of both their newest capabilities and the dangerous and evil forces in the world, and for that matter, the universe as well."

The assault on our unique abilities may also be true regarding those from outside our earth, such as Mr. Xilx and Elizabeth Sam. They may not be aware of the wiles and thoughts individuals on our earth can propagate. Man may well be a very unusual creature to them because of our inventive imaginations and creative abilities.

Mr. Xilx and Elizabeth both took umbrage to these words. Both were extremely displeased at the mere thought that they could do anything evil.

"Now see here, you, whatever your name is, both Elizabeth and I have never even *tried* to overpower the minds of any individual, either on the planet Ida or here on Earth or even elsewhere, and we have been to many 'elsewheres'. Now mind you," Mr. Xilx said staring sternly and while shaking long finger at Walter he added, "We have no agreement with such tactics. We are honest, straightforward, and true." Xilx demanded, "Now you please apologize!"

Walter's surprise at this sudden and unexpected reaction was apparent. Despite his ability to read thoughts, both Mr. Xilx and Elizabeth apparently circumvented Walter's unique talents to read thoughts. He wondered why he had no mental warning on the sudden protest. Were the extra-terrestrials' mind processes so fast that the mind-thought process either never reached Walter's mind or they were able to cloak their thoughts in an instant? It was either that or Walter's abilities were not as good as he believed.

While that thought was circling around in his now puzzled brain, Walter said, "Mr. Xilx and Elizabeth, I did not mean either one of you as I know that you both are only good, honest and want only what is right and just in this world. I am sorry if that phrase offended you.' He then added, "I was referring to others who may be unknown to us at this time. This is a big world and an even bigger universe."

Mr. Xilx and Elizabeth both thought the very same thought: "I'm not sure I accept the apology at all. Walter may have a prejudice against extra-terrestrials."

# CAMERON'S INTRIGUE

Cameron's distant location from the Walter Murphy meeting does not mean that he is not there. It is a quiet afternoon at Cameron's house. He has had all his needs fulfilled and is just laying leisurely about. Perhaps "lazily" is a more appropriate word.

Some people may turn on the radio or television or listen to their favorite music. This is not so with Cameron. His radio, television and music all came out of his interests in the world about him, even when he was at rest.

In Cameron's case, he spends his leisure moments staring into and listening to his companion projected mirror. When nothing is happening, it would make the sound of a mountain breeze and imply calmness and soothing characteristics to its immediate area.

When something is happening, the projected mirror shimmers a bit and then tunes in to whatever is going on. Sometimes more than just one thing is going on and the projection receives it as a static interference. Cameron filters out the different occurrences to suit his taste. No. He does not use halogen light, laser or any other kind of illuminating filter. He instead uses a mental transference filter, which the projected framed mirror receives and interprets. It will then accept only the signals that interest Cameron.

Cameron's attention suddenly turns to his shimmering mirror. It shimmers more violently and displays cloudlike swirls this time, which is a most unusual event. This is way beyond the usual calming mountain wind sound and much beyond the normal, attention-getting wind.

Cameron reacts by quickly rising from his relaxed position and immediately stares into the mirror.

The mirror even changed to multi-color red, brown, yellow and green this time. That event never happened before. Cameron's level of curiosity exceeded all expectations regarding the bowl's messaging center.

"This is most extraordinary. Something quite strange and momentous must be happening, like a multi-continent earthquake or multi-volcanic eruptions or worse," Cameron said aloud on what the mirror's static transmission revealed. His focus brought him into Jack Henigson's living room. The meeting was now fully open, even to Cameron, the proverbial fly on the wall.

Listening in was not easy. Cameron could only get bits and pieces and too much static. What little he heard allowed him to understand that the meeting's purpose is to create a challenge to his abilities to control and use this group.

"Imagine that! The ingrates, and after all they have done for me!"

Cameron became concerned. The comfortable life he had known might be ending. He had difficulty in identifying who was at Henigson's meeting and he could not even identify the meeting place, but he did know why the meeting was happening. He did recognize a threat and that is what the excited mirror was revealing.

Cameron said aloud, "This is bad. It is worse than I thought. Earthquakes and volcanic eruptions would be easier to take. Who are these people?"

It did not take much for Cameron to realize that the only reason for the mysterious group's existence had to be because some of them were his unwitting robotic helpers. If that were the case, then this was a rebellion. He was most certainly right. However, it was more than just a rebellion. It was a resistance movement as well.

"What if this is the start of a world-wide revolution within my entire organization?" Cameron went on, "That is ridiculous. I alone am my organization. I alone control these weak minded, so-called 'gifted', individuals."

His spoken thoughts continued, "But it is obvious that there is resistance. If this turns into a successful resistance movement worldwide, I might have to find a real job. There is no way I will allow that to happen."

Cameron decided to place much effort into discovery. He resolved that he would place more exertion into controlling his robot service agents. In that direction, Cameron would find a quiet place and place himself in a comfortable position because he would be spending many hours entering the minds of his robots in order to reassert his control. He would start immediately.

# HENRY THE DREAMER

The first meeting at Henigson's house was informative with subsequent meetings and instructions scheduled to continue improved resistance to Cameron's influences.

Henry found the session exhausting and he left his friends at Jack's house. He walked home to revive his mind and to get fresh air, however when he arrived at home is just went to bed. His worn out condition made him fall asleep right away. Despite his tiredness, Henry's sleep was restless. He tossed, turned and even sat up while still asleep. He was disturbed. Cameron was again attempting to invade his mind and to gain control of his mind and his body. Henry subconsciously employed some of the techniques he learned at Jack's house. Cameron did not gain entry to Henry's subconscious mind for a change.

When he tried and tried repeatedly, Cameron discovered a strange resistance unlike his earlier successful incursions into Henry's mind.

Cameron felt ill. He thought that perhaps he was coming down with fever. Alas, for Cameron, failure to enter another's mind was devastating. Invading another gifted one's mind took a lot of effort.

The little resistance Henry was able to develop was enough to foil Cameron's attempt at control. This was a new and unpleasant experience for Cameron. He was not coming down with fever, but rather he was experiencing an exhausted and heated body because of failure. He felt like he had a fever, which was false.

Henry, in his restless sleep, dreamt of a tunnel, which was a swirling mass of multiply lined and gossamer threaded with eddies, knots and a whirlpool-like vortex extending into a space above him which was affected by complex interrelationships of magnetism, light, gravity and electricity. There were all kinds of light flashes and sparks all going from one side of the gossamer threaded funnel to the other. The swirl slowly cleared and appeared as a fiber optic cable.

Finally, the sparks and light flashes ceased, and all became quiet. Henry was able to see the other end of the line with some degree of clarity, although minimal, because of the interference of a shimmering mirror's static, like a mistuned radio dial.

Cameron's attempt at invasion turned against him. Henry did not seek to control Cameron but only to discover whatever he could on Cameron's side of the mirror. This was all a part of Walter's initial efforts to help Cameron's victims resist remote mental invasion with only minimal effort while dreaming.

The counter action was all via Henry's subconscious mind and a subliminal desire to succeed. Cameron was not aware that anyone could see him. Cameron's face resided deeply in Henry's subconscious mind. Cameron's surroundings were unforgettably well engraved in Henry's mind. Henry would never forget.

# Chapter Sixteen

# COUNTER-INTELLIGENCE STUDIES

Jack's residence was once more the site of the next meeting. Walter Murphy unceremoniously popped up just as he did the first time in his unhorsed, but cushioned, chariot. He was quickly joined by the Elizabeth and Jack team who also appeared out of nowhere.

Walter was in rare form. He decided that he would lay down the law. His entourage would call it Murphy's Law:

***"Minimal to absolutely no use of telepathic thought was to be permitted, at least for the next several sessions of defensive barrier formation instruction and practice."***

He had no way of knowing whether people are thinking plain ordinary thoughts or are they thinking telepathic thoughts. That was a quandary and one he would like to resolve, that is *if* it could be resolved.

Walter recalled the earlier indignant resentment expressed by Mr. Xilx and his surprised sense of helplessness which he felt because he was not reading and was not forewarned of the thoughts of Elizabeth and Xilx. Mr. Xilx and Elizabeth had to create some type of a defensive barrier which enabled them to prevent the able Walter from reading their thus protected thoughts.

Walter recognized that whatever method they used to cloak their thoughts was exactly what his group of students needed. Walter was eager to explore how they did that and he believed that the rest of them could learn from them and have the group develop the same ability for each group member.

Walter thought to himself, "It would really be a breakthrough if he could get Elizabeth and Xilx to accomplish that!"

The only technique Walter could teach is the "double thought" technique, which is not easy. The double thought method was to think a dominant thought but with a co-dependent sub-liminal thought. It took a lot of practice, but once it was mastered it was easy to throw an eavesdropper off the track and lead him in a different direction all together.

It was something like daydreaming or listening to the radio or a boring speech while your mind is on something entirely different. You heard both. One has your greater attention and the other has a minimally secondary place or hierarchy in your mind.

The question was how to do that consistently and purposefully. It can be confusing when a companion might ask you something about the radio or a boring speech and you respond. "What?" You know, but you really don't know in full consciousness, unless you search your mind and try to recall what that person was really saying. You were distracted because your mind was on a completely different subject. In a sense, you were daydreaming to some extent. You were paying a subliminal attention to the boring event. It was not on the front burner of your mind. That is double thought.

## Chapter Seventeen

# HENRY REACHES OUT AND TOUCHES SOMEONE

Henry went through another sleepless night of disturbed rest because of Cameron's mental invasion attempts. He tossed and turned and even sat up and even opened his eyes, all while asleep. Cameron was once again trying to place his own thoughts into Henry's mind to produce what would be like a so-called post hypnotic suggestion. At one point, Henry could actually hear Cameron's voice suggesting that he should go into a bank or a precious gem jewelry store and teleport either a bunch of $100.00 bills or diamonds of several carats in size.

Unknown to even Henry, he had now developed the ability to transport items of value or not, simply by wishing to do so, any moderate size item from place to place without even placing a hand on it! This questionable "gift" was given to Henry fully unknown and unrealized by Henry.

When the command, or suggestion, came from Cameron for Henry to do so, Henry's unrest came from his personal resistance to perform an act which he felt he was not capable, but also immoral. Henry's sense of honesty helped to make this night's sleep tortuous.

It was this dichotomy of purpose and morality that made this evening's session with Cameron especially unique. After a while Cameron felt that his efforts failed, and he tapered off his attempts to influence Henry. However, this evening, Cameron did not release his mental connection. As in an earlier session, Henry could more clearly see Cameron's face this time as well as hearing his voice.

But there is more. Henry was now able, via Cameron's failing to "hang up" the connection, to see more than just Cameron's face. Henry could see into Cameron's lair, and he was actually able to search out details at Cameron's residence while on an actively "open" connection.

Henry was still strengthening his powers and developing new abilities. Some of these abilities were inadvertently transferred to him by Cameron's attempts to influence Henry's mind. This very act of contact by Cameron resulted in a sloughing off some of Cameron's mental powers. Although it took Cameron many years to "grow" these abilities and which were now inadvertently contaminating Henry. In Henry's case, the so-called "contamination" was becoming part of improved powers for Henry. They were abilities that Henry's associates would not ever develop.

Cameron became tired of the assault on Henry, distracted himself and became involved with a project separate and away from any attempts to continue his assaults on Henry's mind. He left his own residence to perform some mundane errands. Cameron was nowhere to be seen. It was as if on cue with Cameron's loud slamming door that triggered a new response from the still live "connection" with Henry. The "shimmering" mirror image remained in operation.

That was when Henry sat up, although one would consider him to still be asleep. He was, and he wasn't, asleep. Suddenly and remotely out of Cameron's scrying water bowl, which was located near the telepathic mirror, an image arose several thousand miles away from Henry's home. It was a phantom of the young Henry. Henry's subconscious spirit was now sitting up, in the bowl of water, and curiously looking all about Cameron's residence. Henry's body was still at home in bed, although strangely, in a sitting position. Henry's phantom was able to examine all that was within fifty or so feet about him in Cameron's residence and in all directions.

Henry recalled his days with DESE and the all-seeing spectacles. They were part of a collection that Henry was able to assemble. Henry dreamt about them. He dreamt that he would possess them and operate them as they were designed to be surreptitiously used.

He had collected several pairs of these spy spectacles which had the unique ability to adjust themselves to a wearer's optical prescription. Henry dreamt that a pair of his spectacles was on Cameron's desk, and slowly it was so. Then the spectacles we there. They were now physically present in Cameron's apartment for anyone's use. Only one of the pairs of spectacles Henry possessed found their way over the distance of several thousand miles to the exact position Henry dreamt of on Cameron's desk. It was Henry's phantom image which did so.

Cameron's eyes had changed slightly over the years, and he did indeed wear glasses, usually only for reading or for the detailed and close examination of objects of interest.

Henry's spirit slowly "floated" above the scrying bowl and moved across the room. Henry's phantom placed a pair of spying spectacles next to Cameron's desk blotter, looked about, and then faded away only to appear again above Cameron's scrying bowl.

The phantasm, now at the bowl, slowly submerged without a ripple and disappeared. All was quiet. The room was just as Cameron had left it. The only exception was that it had been visited by a stranger several thousand miles away and that Cameron now had a pair of new, very special, harmless looking, but attractively styled spectacles.

## Chapter Eighteen

# Back at Greenwich Avenue Starbucks

Henry is having his own adventures via the scrying bowl at Cameron's home. However, Elizabeth Sam, Jack Henigson, Walter Murphy, and Mr. Xilx are not happy as they do not consider Henry's evening ventures a safe "adventure". They all have intercepted the vicissitudes of Henry's unsettled sleep, and each has melded a mental meeting mission in mind, which is why they have presented themselves here in Walter's home. They are each concerned about Henry's many agonies, every one of which Henry has yet to acknowledge. Henry was not even aware that he had any "agonies". He was only aware that some of his nights were sleepless, but he never realized why.

The group decided to meet at mid-morning at the Greenwich Avenue Starbucks. Walter greeted them with gusto and gratefulness.

He is happy that they all came, each on their own and with mutual respect and genuine concern for Henry.

Walter stepped away for a moment to serve his constant and favorite customer, Tracey Marie, whom he affectionately nicknamed the 'Coffee Queen'. Her regular standing order for Café Quad Grande' with four shots of espresso skim with dry caramel macchiato, but light on caramel was served. (Dry means less milk, more foam. All this was for a reported $5.14).

Tracey Marie thanked Walter graciously and sat down near the group. Just close enough to overhear conversation but far enough away to not overtly impinge on their privacy. Tracey Marie shuffled some of her papers from work and became engrossed with their contents and the last thing that interested her was the meeting nearby. She shortly sped off to get her New York City train.

The meeting was a bit extraordinary, as part of it was vocal, and part of it was mental communiqué. As this Starbucks was Walter's domain, and since it was Walter that made the existence of danger to each of them known, Walter automatically was elected an authority figure and to preside over the gathering as a given.

Walter began, "We all know why we are here. The question is: how to deal with Henry's nightly torture. We are all keenly aware when Henry has his nightly "sessions" because of the mental connection we all have with each other. Some of us have been losing sleep along with Henry, although not to the same extent."

The attendees murmured and nodded in agreement.

"Are there any suggestions as to how we can really help Henry?" Walter asked rhetorically. He went on, ignoring any attempted responses, "When I was much younger, I was also affected by a similar type of problem. I was also unable to "cloak" my thoughts and my mind was an open, revolving door. It was that way for quite a while. I was disturbed by what I thought was basically just simply dreaming and sleepwalking."

"However, it was never a dream or a sleepwalk. I felt that I was just a robot remotely controlled by an evil wizard far away from where I lived.

Mostly he had me committing minor thefts for him and had me place the stolen goods at a pre-directed location which was different each time.

I slowly became aware of what was happening, and I eventually escaped his grip. It was not easy, and I agonized my way through it. I was very lucky because there could be no limit as to where his plans for me were heading. However, his directives could never be the direction I would ever permit myself to go. I resisted and eventually he gave up. I never knew who he was."

"Shortly after Henry's involvement with DESE, I became aware that Henry was pure, innocent and a fertile ground for exploitation, just as I was in my younger days. I intercepted some of Henry's thoughts and knew what was going to happen to him. I could not permit it and that is when I contacted him, and through him, all of you. When I discovered that a mysterious force was making attempts to enter his mind and to make him do what was against his conscience. It was the same type of force I experienced, and I recognized it immediately. Thus, I made contact with Henry as soon as I realized what would be happening to him. None of our 'gifted' colleagues should be permitted to be taken advantage of that way. Believe me. I know."

Walter continued in a near tirade, waving arms and walking around the table where his companions sat.

"The conflicts of conscience, the lack of restful sleep, the unexplainably strangely wet shoes and clothing in the morning after an evening of subconsciously doing the bidding of an evil influence is all unbearable. Henry needs our help, and we all need to get back to our peaceful existence. We need sleep and rest too, but we cannot get that without solving Henry's dilemma."

' His mind projects all that is happening to him, but is also affecting all our minds as we are an interconnected network for good. It is almost as though each of us is going on his semiconscious deeds with him. We need to help Henry because that is the only way we can help ourselves. We need to find the source of whoever is causing Henry's, and our, distress. It is a matter of mutual self-preservation."

Walter stopped, either because he was out of breath or energy.

Jack Henigson intervened with, "Walter, Walter, just calm down. Nothing is to be gained by histrionics. Let us all calmly reason this thing out."

Mr. Xilx joined in, "Of course. Reasoning things out is all we can do. It is obvious at this point that for us to get any peace is to help Henry deal with this aggressive dilemma which has struck him. However, it may be that it is up to Henry to resolve the matter himself. But I do not think <u>we</u> can survive this stress. We must strive to help him somehow."

Elizabeth added, "Of course. No doubt about it. I think that we need to calm Walter down and slowly explore his past experience and how he managed to escape the hold this "X" individual's influence on him. Perhaps we can encourage Henry to do the same."

## CHAPTER NINETEEN

# CAMERON RETURNS HOME

Cameron now enters his San Francisco apartment. His existence is lonely. Cameron is a loner despite his mostly unwilling and unknowing army of pseudo-agents all over the world. None of them are his voluntary friends. He has few friends.

He has amassed a moderately great fortune, large but not great enough to attract attention from the government or its tax agencies. He now only stepped out to get some fresh air and a bit of exercise. He did not even walk a mile. There was something troubling him and he was trying to get a grip on whatever it might be.

The fresh air and the walk helped him, and he became aware of what his problem was, although it was not immediately obvious to him before his walk. The problem was Henry. Henry had developed powers which prevented him from continuing him as a "tool" and robot to Cameron's will and commands.

That disturbed Cameron to no end. Henry was the only remote agent able to resist Cameron's demands. But that was not so; Cameron recalled that some several dozen or so years ago there was another "agent" he remotely controlled who had inexplicably developed the same type of immunity to Cameron's commands. It turns out that was Walter Murphy, now Henry and his cohort's tutor. That was when Cameron was a much younger man and more able to take rejection. Cameron is not happy about Henry.

This is a time in the older Cameron's life when he hopefully expected to be able to relax and enjoy the "finer" things and be involved in pleasant relaxation, enjoying the "fruits" of his remote thievery. Henry's resistance put Cameron in a worrisome state, a disturbing puzzlement.

Cameron thought, "What if my other "agents" became able to resist my commands as well?" This thought kept Cameron on edge. He would have to change his somewhat boring, though comfortable, lifestyle. That would be something he would not like to do.

He moseyed about his apartment for a while and then unceremoniously plopped down at his desk. He shuffled through some papers. He picked up the attractive spectacles on his desk. He did not remember buying them but assumed that he simply forgot about any purchase. Cameron surmised that perhaps these spectacles were one of the "fruits" of his thieving lifestyle.

He never guessed that they were a surreptitious "gift" from Henry, his unwilling, distant, resistant and now rebellious agent. In a way Cameron was now the "innocent" dupe of Henry, although there was nothing "innocent" about him. He was only unsuspecting. He was a thief.

Henry now has virtually turned the tables on Cameron.

Suddenly and without warning, an unexpected and intrusive "wave" of a "gifted", but uninvited telepathic thought enters picture. It is a broadcast to all members of the Starbucks DESE "Gifted Persons Club" directly from the President of the United States.

No one could ever have believed that the President was of the "gifted" club, especially as his more conventional and publicly obvious talents and abilities cloaked his "real" gifts. The "gifts" were the same ones Henry and his immediate "associates" enjoyed but with some extra trimmings and it all makes sense. After all, it is only the president and vice president that share knowledge of the existence of DESE, and this information is passed on only from president to president. In this case, it is a "plus" that the president happens to be one of the "gifted".

The President's telepathic broadcast was cloaked and meant only for the entire and exclusive Starbucks DESE group. The President had fully mastered the technique of "double thought" which basically encrypted mental communication only to those meant to receive the communiqué. The message instructed the group to meet at Jack Henigson's house.

Jack's house was deemed a "safe" house.

## Chapter Twenty

# PRESIDENTIAL MESSAGE

When we think, our thoughts are processed in our most native language. These thoughts usually stay within our head, except in the case of inexperienced "gifted" persons where a thought may be inadvertently "shared" among gifted members and associates. The exception is when one knows how to cloak those thoughts through "double-think". Such is the case with Henry. He is in the process of perfecting the "double-think" mechanism and is almost there.

The group assembled at Jack's residence as the president directed. The assemblage was present for less than a split second before they were treated to the presidential telepathic "video" presence. There was the usual flash of light, a cloud of phantasmal dust and a hearty "hi-ho" came from the president. It reminded one of the old Lone Ranger days of "Hi-ho Silver, Up, Up and Away!" But of course, this was much more serious as it comes from the President of our United States!

The President raised himself up from his chair behind the Oval Office desk and leisurely sat on the front of it, assuming a more congenial pose.

"He began, "I am happy to meet with you. We are all very fortunate to be "gifted", as the term goes. Of course, this is only known to us and no one outside this very special circle. Not even the vice president knows of our unique abilities."

He continued, "I am especially fortunate, as the first member of my ethnic background to be in this unique office, an office which only few are able to attain. Nevertheless, along with this office go a greater number of responsibilities than anyone who does not achieve it can ever know. But I do not want to go there. "

You are all members of the Department of Extraordinary Situations and Events, or DESE, as we call it for short. What I must inform you is not a surprise. We all know of the threat of terrorism. We feel that we also know the threat of economic collapse and the loss of our financial position in the world. However, we still have initiative and opportunity that virtually does not exist anywhere else in the world.

That opportunity shows itself in many different ways. It shows in discovery, inventiveness, persistence, fortitude, courage and business, as well as many other fields of endeavor. Unfortunately, it may also show itself in the field of greed and theft.'

The president paused for a short, but emphatic, moment as he has been known to do. Continuing, he said pedantically, "You all know that our country is in a financial crisis. Our currency is weaker against those of other nations, although we are holding our own and making modest headway against further weakening.

You know that in the 1970s we took our currency off the gold backing of our currency and replaced it with silver backing. That was not enough. We then decided that the full faith and credit of our country was enough to keep our currency and our country competitive with the rest of the world. That was so for many decades, nearly a century.

However, we still have a more than just adequate but a very sizeable store of gold. Fort Knox is well known for the storage of gold for instance. But something curious is happening. Every so often a bar of gold disappears, into thin air as it were. No one sees it go. No one enters the storage area. There are no openings other than vents, and everything is monitored every minute of every day.

Such a matter as this must be under the definite purvey of the DESE. This is truly an Extraordinary Situation and Event indeed! It is as though the bar vanishes in thin air! No one has been able to explain such events."

This was an emphatic announcement, especially with the President pounding his fist on his desk out of frustration and standing up in the same moment. This was truly a crisis event at the White House level.

Everyone in the meeting room at Jack's house was silent, but their thoughts were running rampant. Fortunately, some of the laws contained in Walter Murphy's lessons had sunk in and their thoughts did not leave their heads or the room.

The President now stood silently, glaring at the audience, as he could see them too. He was waiting for a response. He waited and waited.

The group mumbled and said nothing. And the President still waited there, standing and staring.

## Chapter Twenty-One

# THOUGHTS, CONTEMPLATION AND EXPLORATION

The president was still standing there.

Something was happening. A figure arose from the midst of the group and came forward toward the Presidential viewing area.

Jack Henigson addressed the President, "Mr. President", he began, "You are correct when you say that the events as you describe are well within the scope of DESE, the Department of Extraordinary Situations and Events. The vanishing of material objects into thin air is sometimes a trick of magic, but since you are one of us, the gifted ones, you realize that this is not magic, nor a trick. The Treasury is being robbed via events which indeed are extraordinary.

The President responded, "Of course I realized the virtual supernatural character of the occurrence. After several heavy bars of gold disappeared without notice and from under intense security, it became apparent that unnatural forces were behind the thefts. The vaults are always well sealed and guarded by many means. I know of no better group of people to investigate this than all of you as members of DESE and DESE itself as a secret government agency."

Continuing the President added, "There were similar instances of such theft in England regarding certain gems removed from the Crown Jewels and Scepter. These disappearances were never solved. However, that is a matter for England and Scotland Yard.

I am most concerned with the lost gold from our very secure vaults. Please get on the case and let me know what you learn. Should it become news and revealed to the world that the United States is losing its gold the value of our currency and other commodities could become radically changed."

The President then unceremoniously disappeared, without so much as a goodbye or anything like that. One minute he was there and the next he was gone. There was no flash-bang. Just disappearance. Perhaps something like the vanishing gold of his concern.

No one was surprised at the sudden termination of the communication. Such communications are always at risk of interception.

Jack Henigson, Mr. Xilx, Elizabeth, and Henry had their mental wheels turning incessantly. Henry was the first to break the silence.

"Very easy", Henry said confidently. "It is simple material teleportation."

Mr. Xilx observed, "But of course. There is a problem with your theory."

Jack intervened, "It is that teleportation involves the physical movement of an item. The question is: How did the physical mass of gold get through the walls to whatever destination it made?"

Elizabeth said, "It had to be more than just teleportation. The gold bar had to be vaporized and be turned into some kind of a virtual "spiriting away". How else could a solid, heavy gold bar disappear? The real question is "how"?

That question put them all into a very deep silence. They all looked at each other questioningly.

They were all thinking, "How indeed?"

## Chapter Twenty-Two

# BACK IN HIS LAIR

Cameron is comfortable in his large soft leather lounger. He is sitting back and reading a book on theoretical molecular changes and transitions. He is quite a content loner. He is comfortable with his own presence and has minimal need for any kind of companionship.

The book's title is "Molecular Vaporization of Alkanes, Silicon and Germanium", a research report. Cameron is an avid, quick reader. He rapidly assimilates the information and is finished in short order.

He thought to himself, "These substances and this vaporization study is really child's play. The authors should know all that I know. They would be quite amazed and surprised indeed!"

He then puts the book aside with a contemptuous sneer, opens the cabinet near his desk and peers in with delight. In the cabinet are four bars of gold stamped with the seal of the U.S. Treasury and numbers revealing the bar's 99.99% purity. He smiled and laughed a short laugh to himself, and then closed the cabinet door.

Cameron recalled that youthful event many years ago, when he turned the double-headed coin to reveal the obverse side of a normal coin, namely the "tail". That event even surprised him. He had no idea he had that ability. He reflected that this was just the beginning of things to come.

He recalled how he was able to remove precious stones from the royal English scepter in the very presence of security and guards. They were no match for him or his powers.

He is now more advanced in the dissolution into ethers, or gases, of solid material objects. The removal of the British gems was only a testing ground for bigger things to come. The gems were small and not heavy. Their transport into his possession was relatively easy.

Cameron sought advancement to bigger and more challenging things. The presence of the United States' gold bars in his cabinet was his latest achievement. He was quite satisfied with himself. The challenge was not so much his "willing" the bars to physically change their molecular structure to a gaseous vapor, but in how the transportation of the now gaseous bars could possibly pass though the ventilation appurtenances of the secure vaults and into his hands, so many miles away and then recompose, at Cameron's will, into the original gold bar which began the voyage.

Initially he found the effort quite exhausting, but that is no longer any problem. He now performs the task with ease. The transport and disintegration of gold into a vapor and the moving of that item, intact as a gaseous mass, a distance of several thousand miles, is a crowning achievement. Cameron is now quite secure in his own being and has no fear of ever being caught as the thief he really is.

Cameron sees the matter as a challenge and not really thievery. It is now accomplished, and Cameron is losing interest.

He is not aware that there are "eyes" all around him.

## Chapter Twenty-Three

# HENRY'S DREAMS

Henry left the meeting at Jack's house feeling quite disturbed. He found the directive presented by the President very challenging. He reflected on his own disturbed nights, those nights when he felt an invading mental presence. One to which he could not make any connection or anything sensible. The invasion was as vague as vague could be.

Henry also realized that he had fewer of those dreams in the present than he experienced in the past.

"It must be Walter Murphy's instructions and influence that helped me", he thought.

It was a good guess, but only a guess. The fact was that Henry's personal morals and his innate recognition of evil and wrongdoing was the mechanism by which he resisted Cameron's attempts at control and mental invasion.

Henry also found the "meeting" at Jack's house physically exhausting; all that thinking and double thought transference was tiring.

Henry went home to his parents who did not suspect anything unusual. They never did. Henry behaved as normal and helped with the dishes after dinner and soon thereafter bid his parents "good night".

It did not take the tired Henry much time before he went to bed. He kept the Medallion Walter originally snuck into Henry's suitcase and it always hung on the bedpost at the head of his bed.

Tonight was different. That night the medallion awoke with a glow exactly when Henry began his slumber and started snoring away in REM sleep. Walter, in the medallion, turned about to see Henry. Walter watched over him as he slept for part of the night. Walter was worried about Henry and the mysterious mental invader whose incursion into Henry's mind and which Henry strenuously and constantly resisted, sometimes causing Henry to awaken in a more tired condition than when he went to sleep. This was because of Henry's effort to resist Cameron.

But tonight was different. Tonight, Henry was not alone. Walter was with him in more ways than one.

Walter could see Henry asleep. Walter could also "hear" Henry's thoughts and read his mind. On the other hand, Walter could also witness and assess the assault by Cameron, who remained unknown to Walter, as he attempts constant invasion into Henry's mind.

Cameron was not going to give up "control" of the Henry robot so easily. Cameron didn't have any inkling that this particular night Henry was not alone. Cameron unwittingly had a double battle to confront. Walter was Henry's ally and Cameron was in for a surprise this evening. It would not be an evening "as usual" in Cameron's attacks on Henry.

Cameron was as stubborn as stubborn could be. He stared deeply and intensely into the scrying bowl. Its surface rippled and increased its rippling intensity as Cameron's efforts to reach Henry's mind increased. Nonetheless, Cameron increased his efforts, and the ripples were turning into waves within that scrying bowl. There was now the beginning of a virtual whirlpool being produced; Cameron's mental powers were so intense.

Walter was reading Henry's mind. He watched as Henry tossed and turned; now producing a severe sweat because of his resistance.

Then something happened. Not with Henry but at Cameron's residence. The transported spectacles developed eyeballs. Both Henry and Walter were now able to actually see Cameron in his effort to assault Henry. As they both watched, Henry in his subconscious mind, and Walter as an ally, observing all through Henry's mind. Walter was able to basically "draw a bead" on Cameron.

With almost insurmountable effort, the spectacles on the desk turned and looked about Cameron's residence. Walter spied the cabinet which held the gold bars. Walter "willed" the cabinet's doors to open and he moved one of the heavy bars via teleportative influence.

At first the bar resisted, but Walter augmented his mental effort to the point where he also was perspiring. The bar moved further and was now out of the cabinet but suspended in midair. With an additional Herculean effort, Walter willed that the bar fly across the room and its target was Cameron's head. Henry really was not aware of his remotely controlled mind by the now beneficent Walter Murphy.

There was Cameron. His eyes nearly squinted shut in response to his own super effort to enter Henry's mind only to meet constant and increasing resistance. He was still puzzled as to how this young individual could resist the mental telepathic powers and strength of the unfailing master, Cameron.

Then it hit him. No, it was not the reason why Henry could resist him, but rather Cameron was hit by the flying gold bar. Because of the bar's weight and flying speed, Cameron was knocked out cold. He fell forward into the scrying bowl which suddenly stopped rippling and spilled a bit. The mental cause for Henry's disturbed sleep was gone. Cameron was no longer producing telepathy towards Henry because he was out cold. All Cameron's mind's efforts were blank. The communication was broken. The remaining water in the bowl was unmoving. There was not a ripple.

Henry immediately fell into a comfortable sleep and his perspiring waned as did Walter's. All was now at peace for this evening at least for Henry and all his friends.

## Chapter Twenty-Four

# AWAKENING

It was the next morning when Cameron saw daylight. He was dazed and not immediately able to fully understand as to what happened and why he was not in bed.

He was amazed that he was on the floor in front of the scrying bowl which was partially emptied. He did not recall why it was askew.

He sat up. He did not like being prone on the floor and all his joints and bones ached. He sighed and stretched. The biggest pain he had was in his head. A tremendous headache, almost like a migraine was what he felt and with a swollen lump!

Cameron reflected, "If all this pain and agony were not enough then why is that gold brick on the floor? How did it get there?"

"Oh my gosh!" he exclaimed. "I've been robbed!" he screamed. "The robbers must not have been able to carry this extra gold brick! All the bars had to be too heavy for them! They must have slugged me!"

The next thing he sought out was the cabinet where he kept his stolen gold bars.

"Strange", he thought. "Nothing seems to be missing, but the cabinet door is open!"

Cameron mused a bit and slowly his memory cleared, and all came back to him.

He remembered the scrying bowl! He remembered the extra effort he put into invading Henry's mind! He remembered the extreme rippling of the water at the bowl's surface, almost to the point of violence!

Then he realized that he remembered nothing; nothing at all. It was all black until he awoke this morning. Even then it took him time to put the last evening's adventure together. Even now, he was not certain. But he did have suspicions. It was all a guess. There were no facts beyond the scrying bowl spill and the gold brick on the floor.

"Henry!" he exclaimed. "It had to be Henry's doing, but how?"

Cameron only had suspicions, guesses and nothing more to go on.

## CHAPTER TWENTY-FIVE

# THE OTHER SIDE OF THE COIN

After Cameron lost contact with Henry, Henry was able to sleep soundly. Walter knew what had happened; Henry would only remember it as a foggy dream, soon to be forgotten upon awakening as the details of dreams seem to fade away.

The medallion which hung by Henry's bedpost was still there but no longer glowing.

All of Henry's associates, meaning all those who inadvertently were in Henry's mental telepathic circle, also finally had a good night's sleep. All his friends at DESE were very grateful. None knew what or why, but they all needed the rest, for when Henry's sleep was disturbed by Cameron's invasions, they all were telepathically disturbed as well.

Only one person really knew the real story. That person was Walter Murphy.

Walter kept thinking about his early years which were similarly disturbed. He was beginning to draw parallels between his past and the present. Henry's experiences were too familiar.

Walter was not going to let this familiarity disappear from his life so easily. He was still very much disturbed by his past. It was something he would never forget and if he should learn who his assailant was, he would not forgive just as he could never forget.

He was determined to learn if whoever caused his distress years ago was the same entity which caused Henry's current disturbance and the connecting disturbances of all his fellow telepaths. He had faith that under the current circumstances that the villain would eventually be uncovered. He had faith that whoever was foolish to do this when a network of fellow telepaths were involved that the perpetrator would make some incriminating errors. Walter, now an adult calmly "reasoned it out".

# KNOWING DISCOVERY

Transportation of physical items through space was no mystery to Cameron. It all began in his younger days when his ability to make the red lights which slowed his automobile transportation changed to green as his car approached. It was an ability which Cameron did not know he had. As a matter of fact, Cameron was not sure that his simply wishing for a green light had anything to do with his ease through traffic.

The changing of the double-headed coin from heads to tails in the magic store was the first real clue for Cameron, but he did not really take that seriously. He felt it was just a fluke. Just something that happened and he never gave the matter a second thought.

It was on a trip to Rincon, Puerto Rico that clinched the fact that he had the ability to change physically into whatever he wanted. He suspected that he was able to make the physical change according to his will. He convinced himself during his visit to the Rincon Puntas area.

He was staying at a place near Vista Linda overlooking a lighthouse in the distance. Cameron's continued staring at the constant spinning light was mesmerizing and Cameron floated off into almost unconscious thought. The hypnotic effect deepened as he continued watching the light house, El Faro.

The nighttime beam rotated clockwise. Cameron thought, "These lights almost always rotate clockwise. I wonder if I can make it go counterclockwise." He intensified his thoughts for a fraction of a second. El Faro just stopped, as though it was stuck or "thinking", then it resumed its course. But this time it went counterclockwise.

"Interesting.", thought Cameron. "Nonetheless these lights are always white. The airport lights are green and white. Wouldn't it be something if this light turned to a red and green color as well."

No sooner than his thought was completed, the light darkened for almost a full minute. It then resumed its counterclockwise travel with a green light changed to red every other time it made its full 360-degree rotation.

Cameron was astounded. He could not believe his eyes. He was convinced that his thought actually changed the distant physical object to his own likings. He then wondered if he could simply ask that the changes he had just caused could be reversed.

In one second, they were. It appeared instantaneously.

The Rincon experiment worked. Cameron went on to bigger and better things. He studied the new science of Noetics and learned how to influence the physical matter all around him. He was a gifted student and he learned much more than the simple lessons he was taught. After all, Noetics is still in its infancy.

Cameron was way ahead of the average "gifted" man's mental threshold of thought and brain power. He could have taught Noetics and contributed major advancements in man's abilities regarding futuristic thinking. However, he chose to keep his abilities secret and to himself, or so he thought.

He was not really cognizant of DESE and the "gifted" individuals that made up its membership or the unusual quality of any individual member of the DESE organization, with emphasis on one very special member, Henry Wilson.

## Chapter Twenty-Seven

# NOETICS AND CAMERON

Still in its infancy, and requiring continuing exploration, double blind studies, experimentation and acceptance in the general scientific community, Noetics has its place.

It most certainly has its place in Cameron Schulz's life. He was an unknowing and differently "gifted" individual and in many ways he was special. His "gift" was never recognized by him as "gift" and Cameron still, to this day, never recognized it as such. He thought that it is what it is and nothing more. To him it was nothing special and he presumed that he was not unique.

Cameron could have used his special mental abilities to do many beneficial services for the betterment of mankind. That thought never occurred to him. He felt that he was denied so much by society and that his needs were never met. As a result, his efforts were centered on satisfying those needs. He never achieved satisfaction no matter how much he gleaned of earthly matter and things.

He instead used the science of thought and prayer and thought control and special genetic characteristics to his own, self-centered, selfish end.

He never heard of quantum mechanics and anything of other investigations and theories of Albert Einstein. Cameron never suspected that a condition of "quantum entanglement" ever existed, much less the idea of "nonlocality".

Cameron was an unknowing expert at implementing both the working conditions of quantum entanglement's nonlocality. It is what allowed him to perform feats that may appear "magical" to some, but just a scientific reality to those who had knowledge of the two conditions and their connections. Both of those connections were theoretical but in Cameron's case the theory was reality. It was not only reality, but Cameron put the realities of quantum entanglement and nonlocality into practical use. It was a "gift" with which Cameron was born, thus the double headed coin trick became a reality in his youth. His use of these theories was incredibly developed in his mind and improved with the passage of time. His mental abilities were beyond simply being extraordinary. They were, to the average person on the street, simply "magic".

Experiments in Noetic research at CERN laboratories in Geneva substantiated the quantum entanglement idea of nonlocality. As a result, these experiments in a way, and as a corollary, substantiate Albert Einstein's idea that all matter is really a form of "energy".

Albert Einstein supposedly felt that the scientific world was wrong about what matter is. The belief is that matter is really a form of energy where "vibrations" are slowed becomes a probable fact. The slowed energy molecular vibrations produce what we "see" as matter. We can see it. We can touch it. We can move it. We can change it.

Undoubtedly Einstein wasn't considering the sole use of "brain power" to accomplish change. Cameron was in the process of mastering the projection of mental power to cause changes in physical substances. He was now doing it!

That is what Noetics is all about.

This is where Cameron is way ahead in the physical sciences. Whether or not the powers with which Cameron was born and presently displays is an inheritance from theoretical Pleiadian ancestry or not, is a matter for contemplation. In any case, it is a power which he owns and uses.

It is a power that he controls, and his abilities have increased and improved as Cameron matured. Indeed, Cameron is uniquely powerful and virtually superhuman, although he really feels inadequate in life. His contributions to society and those few around him were minimal to nonexistent.

His best relationship was with his pet rock and the bars of gold in his cabinet. His ability to interact with other humans was limited. He did not really have that skill developed, except in mind control. This meant that people around him were not fully free to interact with him, because all he would receive would be a reflection in agreement with his own thoughts just returning to him like a ball bouncing off a wall.

It was different in Henry's case. Here was another "gifted" person whom he could no longer influence. Henry's thoughts were his own. Cameron's thoughts remained as Cameron's thoughts only. None of Henry's abilities ever transferred to Cameron. Henry learned enough cloaking of his own thought to thwart any transfer to Cameron.

Cameron would like to meet this resistant soul, Henry Wilson. Cameron no longer was the master of his fate, at least insofar as Henry was concerned.

Unfortunately for Cameron, his powers were thwarted by an equally, or more, gifted young man namely Henry Wilson, whose sense of morality produced a subconscious resistance to Cameron's thieving "nonlocality" commands. Here the "gifted" Cameron was foiled and became almost irrationally disturbed as a result of his failure.

## CHAPTER TWENTY-EIGHT

# THE DEPARTMENT OF EXTRAORDINARY AND SUPERNATURAL EVENTS RECONVENES

It became a common thought amongst all the closely connected mental-telepathically empowered individuals that they needed to meet to deal with Henry's assailant. Despite the fact that Henry was able to ward off the latest attack and that they were finally all able to get some much-needed sleep. Every one of them realized that this was not the end of Henry's mysterious adventures.

They all wanted it to stop. To that end Mary Kent was notified of the situation by Jack Henigson. Mary agreed and the meeting was scheduled.

Most of the original team nucleus from the first challenge they had against the evil witches were present. There was Jack Henigson, Mr. Xilx, Elizabeth Sam, Seemore and his wife Hepseva, Eddy Erp, (also known as Wyatt), and Henry Wilson. The other members of DESE were not summoned to this meeting. They were not part of the original "nucleus" of which this group consisted.

Henry asked, "Mary, shouldn't we have Walter Murphy here as well? After all, he is the one who started my awareness of the entire problem. He is the one who contacted me right after my return from our last assignment."

Mary answered, "But of course he should be here. Although he is not a part of DESE, all it would take is my saying he should be here and join us as a DESE member."

Henry answered, perfunctorily, "You bet!"

Mary replied, "How can we contact him at this late date? His notice would be short."

Henry answered, "No problem."

He then closed his eyes and added telepathically, "Walter, if you can hear me, you know my thoughts. Would you please arrive at DESE headquarters right away?"

No sooner than he finished the thought that a flaming, horseless chariot appeared out of nowhere and in their midst. There was Walter stepping out of the chariot in the most cavalier manner.

"Henry, thank you for the invite, and you too Ms. Kent."

Mary Kent exhibited all kinds of conflicting emotions. She was shocked at the immediacy of Walter's arrival. She was surprised at the sudden appearance of a flaming chariot out of thin air. She was happy that Walter was present. She was speechless and was just standing there in shock, unable to speak, although her mouth was wide open.

Walter took her hand in his and kissed it. That shocked Mary further. Then he turned his attention to his still flaming chariot and snapped his fingers. The chariot disappeared into thin air.

This, of course, only served to increase the shock value to Mary, who was once again further shocked by the entire event.

Mary stuttered and tried to say, "You, you, you are welcome. I, I, I am happy to have you join us."

"It is my pleasure, Ms. Kent. I would like to be of service and have whoever is influencing Henry either be brought to justice, stop what he is doing or convert him to performing good works instead of whatever he does. He certainly is disturbing the peace in the least", Walter continued with a flair and dignity which rivaled Mrazy Xilx's super noble interstellar decorum.

Walter then turned to all the other attendees, especially Henry, and paid his respects to everyone.

He then turned back to Mary and asked, "What is this Department of Extraordinary and Supernatural Events all about?

Mary was to the limit of her being surprised. She was almost ready to faint, but Jack Henigson intervened and supported her by reinforcing her resistance to a fall by placing his arm about her waist.

Mary quickly recomposed herself and said, "Mr. Murphy, it is what it is. It deals with exactly what its title states. We deal with extraordinary and supernatural events. Your entry here was at the least "extraordinary" in the most conservative sense of the word."

"Ms. Kent, are you inviting me to be a part of this organization?" Walter seized the opportunity to beg the question. He already read Mary's mind and knew in advance of his request that Mary thought, privately to herself, that "this man should most certainly be a part of our organization. His abilities are fantastic, and we need him."

Mary, not being of the "gifted" group, was not aware that her thoughts were being read. She readily answered, "Of course. We need you and your abilities. You are obviously immensely qualified to be a part of our group. Would you accept such and invitation?"

Walter was waiting for such an invite, although he coyly did not respond immediately. Mary waited, somewhat concerned that his answer was not immediate.

He asked, "Ms. Kent, are there dues and other obligations I would have to meet in order to become a member of DESE?"

Mary laughed, "No there are not. However, you will have to swear allegiance to the United States of America, its Constitution and agree not to be destructive in any way to our country. Your qualifications are obvious, and our need is immediate."

Walter responded, "Terrific! I accept the invitation and I will be happy to be a part of a team which is devoted to the good of our nation, its people, its way of life and such. I accept."

The small group cheered and applauded. Walter Murphy was now a part of DESE. Of course, he would still maintain his position at Greenwich Avenue's Starbucks and his new part-time job at the Acadia Coffee House. Walter liked being around people. He enjoyed listening to their stories, problems and expected solutions.

Sometimes he would inadvertently pick up some significant information regarding strange occurrences in the area. That is how he originally picked up on Henry's return from the evil witches' problem and learned how to make contact with Henry via his "enchanted" medallion.

## Chapter Twenty-Nine

# WALTER'S SECRETS

"Well", started Walter, "Let us get down to business."

All looked at Walter intently, expecting that his almost super extraordinary abilities made him an "authority" on the problems facing them. The extended silence which followed was pregnant as each pair of eyes was glued on Walter.

"I ran into a problem like Henry's years ago when I was a young lad, just about like Henry. I was not able to resist commands which entered my sleeping mind. I performed deeds of which I was never fully aware and all in service to this unknown power. Eventually, like Henry, I was able to resist and after several more attempts by this "power" and my continued intent and eventual success in resistance, I was able to dispel the invasion into my subconscious. It ceased."

"However, the recurrence of the very same events involving Henry reawakened the memory of my past. I decided that here was an opportunity for me to redeem myself from the actions which compelled me in the past. Here was an opportunity for me to learn who or what this mysterious 'power" was and to achieve some type of justice or solution. It was then that I contacted Henry. It was through Henry that I am now in the presence of, and a new, eager member of DESE. Together we will successfully fight this 'force' and finally defeat it."

Walter continued, "Henry was able to defeat attempts to influence his subconscious at an earlier age than I. Together Henry and I will terminate these nighttime invasions into the subconscious. Of course we will all, as a group, each aid in the defeat of whatever this 'force' is."

The silent pause was once again expectant. They waited for Walter to continue, but he remained silent, awaiting some feedback from the DESE grouping.

"What we need now is a bit of "brainstorming", but not telepathically, otherwise we will not understand what each of us is trying to 'think'!", said Walter as he organized the gifted grouping.

All was silent as each member of the group thought to themselves and examined whatever they might be able to imagine would work against this mysterious, invading foreign force. It did not remain silent for very long.

Henry became excited and blurted out "I know! I know!"

All were now focused on Henry.

Henry explained, "In my sleep I remember that I actually visited the place from which this 'force' emanates. I remember seeing the actually room, all in a dream".

While each person was intrigued and attentive, some scoffed and said, "But Henry, it was only a dream! You can't rely on dreams!"

Henry retaliated, "No. It was much more than a dream. There was a scrying bowl. I followed the emanations from whoever was using it backwards to their "place of business" as it were. I saw the place! I saw the place!" Henry repeated for emphasis.

Walter became very interested, more so than the others who were all very interested as well.

"Tell us, Henry. Tell us everything you saw." Walter encouraged Henry's story. "But don't embellish it, please."

Henry replied, "Indeed I won't. It is a story which will need no embellishment at all!"

"Go on", said Walter along with the others in eager unison.

"I saw myself rising out of this large bowl of water. I actually walked about the room, which was not very large, but comfortably outfitted. I saw some gold bars in a cabinet and a very nice, functional desk!", Henry explained.

"So?" asked Walter. "Did you see anyone? Did you get any idea of where you were? Did you see any notes? Did you read anything? Did you see any pictures or posters that might give us an idea of where you might have been?"

Henry was sheepish and looked down. His excitement faded, but only for a moment because he did not see any of those things. He had no idea of where he was or what the assailant looked like. He had absolutely no clue whatsoever.

He conveyed that to the group, all of whom also felt lost. A bit of information was near at hand, but nothing to hang a hat or a scarf on.

In the midst of this disappointment Henry once again perked up excitedly.

"Wait. Wait. I remember that I placed a pair of "All Seeing Spectacles" on his desk. I don't know what possessed me to do that, but I did do it! I had three pairs at home and now I only have two. I <u>know</u> that the third pair is at the "wherever" it might be."

The "All Seeing Spectacles" were truly at the "Wherever" place. All became excited, except for Mary Kent. She was not happy that DESE equipment was not where it should be, back at DESE headquarters.

Mary's dark side faded as she realized that the presence of the "All Seeing Spectacles" at the "enemy's" camp was a real plus. All DESE had to do was to monitor and even "spy" on the "Whomever" Mr, "X" who was un-nameable for the moment. The mysterious person or persons or agency would soon become known as well as where in the world he, they or it was located. Soon the forces of DESE would be mobilized to end the sleepless night invasions and illegal deeds that went with them.

Each gave each other the "high five" and gloom turned into satisfied pleasure.

# CHAPTER THIRTY

# SURVEILLANCE

For some reason, the nighttime attacks ceased, at least for a short while. Sleep and recovery for each member of the group who was in "tune" with Henry's mental telepathic frequency were now able to sleep, including Henry.

They each realized that they basically had the "resolution" of their problem and that it was only a matter of time that they would soon "catch" whatever the force was which caused them all so much misery. That was enough to allow them some mental relaxation. They were all somewhat worn out. A good night's rest was what each needed.

Each member was assigned a certain "watch" period on the "All Seeing Spectacles" monitors. It was not long before they each had something to report. Then it would be a small task to put all the bits and pieces of information together and locate the mysterious "force".

The main watchers were Jack Henigson, Mr. Xilx, Elizabeth Sam, Seemore Manlein, Henry and Mary Kent. Since they had no idea from where in the world the controlling emanations came, they instituted a twenty-four-hour watch, at least until they could get a handle on the source. That means each had a four-hour watch assignment. Assignments were made according to age, the hour within the day's clock, and the busyness of each, separately.

The hours began at midnight, Washington, DC time on a Friday night. It was reasoned that whatever the source, a weekday might involve daily obligations on the part of this foreign source and thus a weekend might be better. Fortunately, this group made the decision to surveillance on a Thursday. That meant the next day would be the first time they would be watching for their culprit, culprits or organization that might be off a daily workday and had time to "play" with innocent victims possibly around the world.

The first to watch would be Henry, then Elizabeth Sam, both in the wee hours of the evening. Then at 8:00 AM Mary Kent would be on duty, followed by Mr. Xilx, Seemore Manlein and Jack Henigson to finish the first twenty-four-hour watch.

The hours most dreaded were the lonely hours from 12:00 AM midnight to 4:00 AM. However, the dreading did not have to take place for very long. It was Seemore Manlein who got the first glimpse of one perpetrator. At first, he thought his eyes were playing tricks on him, because all he saw was a newspaper. A printed news article was appearing on the screen, line by line. It was as though a regular television station was broadcasting news, but by the printed page. Seemore was next to being stunned. Here was an "All Seeing Spectacles" device which was transmitting the news! Indeed! Seemore was beginning to get angry. He suspected that he was being played for a fool. "This had to be some kind of trick", he said aloud to himself.

He soon realized that he was mistaken, and the pages faded away into to the top of a desk and it was closed. The top page read "San Francisco Chronicle". Seemore had struck gold! The location of the malevolent source had been located. He was beside himself with joy.

That joy became short lived because as the "Chronicle" was put down, another paper's cover appeared. It was titled "Chicago Tribune" and under that was the "Sun-Sentinel" followed by the "Greenwich Post" in Greenwich, CT. Seemore realized that while DESE was surveying the "source", the same "source" was surveying other parts of the United States and probably more.

This did not please Seemore. He thought that he "had" the malicious source, but apparently not. Whoever or whatever this source was, it had nationwide intentions and was gathering "intelligence" from different parts of the country to learn what events, financial institutions and more were a possible source for thievery.

"Damn!" he exploded. "Damn, damn, damn, damn!" Seemore was angry as well as disappointed, but in his disillusionment, he swore that he would put even more effort into catching whoever or whatever this malicious source was. He became more determined than ever and kept on post, watching for more clues as to where this "X" factor might be found. He, and others would refer to this unknown as "X".

## Chapter Thirty-One

# "X" Factor Continued

Apparently, a case of quantum entanglement occurred; Mr. X continued his perusal of newspapers and coincidentally, a "Greenwich Post" newspaper also was present at the "All Seeing Spectacles" monitoring site that was now monitored by Jack Henigson after a shift change with Seemore leaving.

"X" picked up that paper. It was the same current edition that Jack Henigson had next to the monitor. "X" turned the pages and stopped at the page which announced that there would be a polo match at the Polo Club at Conyers Farm in Greenwich, CT at which Prince William of England, currently the Duke of Cambridge, would be playing. Prince William is a near expert at polo playing and enjoyed it immensely.

Jack Henigson picked up his copy and turned to the same page. It did not take Jack long to understand why "X" kept his copy opened to the same page. Greenwich is one of the wealthiest parts of the nation. All types of people, especially rich ones, would be attending the polo match and gatherings thereafter. It would be a very ripe opportunity for "X" to have a gathering of his own.

"X" planned on it. "X" planned on attending in person this time. He could still get his mentally controlled "robots" to do his bidding and still reap ill-gotten gains. Since "X" did not have many friends in the area, he still liked the idea of mingling among the more fortunate, especially the wealthy and famous. Here was an opportunity to reap and enjoy near exotic company. The "exotic" did not do much for him, but "wealthy exotic" did and that is where he was headed.

Using the spectacles he came to like very much, the "All Seeing Spectacles", he prepared his journey to the East coast and planned to travel by air.

He went to his computer and, while still wearing his favorite glasses, sought out the Air Tran site. He would make his arrangements and that would reveal facts which Jack Henigson would "pounce" upon immediately.

There it was: From SFO Air Tran Flight 322 to HPN Flight 660 with one stop at ATL Flight 661 where "X" would change planes.

It was done! Jack now knew from where "X" was coming. He could tell, as the "All Seeing Spectacles" revealed, that "X" was at his own residence by the books and bed and bath, et cetera, that this is where he lived. This was the home of "X"!

The best part of it all was that he now also knew "X's" residence, and time of arrival.

"Now," Jack thought to himself, if I could get to see what he looks like. I need to see his face!"

Jack was striking gold on what was the fourth shift of the first day of surveillance.

Jack did not really expect to learn what "X's" face looked like especially because "X" removed his "All Seeing Spectacles" and placed them on his desk near his computer.

Jack once again struck gold!

"X" liked his "All Seeing Spectacles" so much that he was careful to not place them with the lenses down on the desk lest they become scratched. He left them on his desk with the arms opened and the lenses facing out.

This was ideal for Jack. One recalls that a feature of the "All Seeing Spectacles" is that not only could a distant observer "read" and "see" what the user sees and reads, but that, from a distance of thousands of miles away, the distant observer, in this case Jack Henigson, could also use those very same glasses to look through them as well. That is exactly what Jack did!

After "X" made his reservations online he stepped away from his desk. The glasses were still as he positioned them, facing outward and resting upside down with their arms opened to avoid scratching.

Jack let a few moments pass because he did not want "X", whose name was no longer unknown, to observe what would be happening next. Then Jack went into action.

Jack remotely placed his own eyes behind the "All Seeing Spectacles" lenses. There was the most eerie sight! A pair of glasses with no one wearing them but with a pair of eyeballs therein, looking out and around!

It took Jack a few moments to adjust because he was as shocked as anyone would be at what was happening!

He was able to actually see Cameron Schulz's face and he "clicked" the photo capture button on the monitor to record the image. He did it again and again, just to be sure he captured Schulz's image. Cameron Schulz is now caught, although his place of residence remained a mystery. It would not be long before Schulz would be caught!

## Chapter Thirty-Two

# BACK AT DESE HEADQUARTERS

It did not take long for Jack to spread the news. All the select agents, including Henry assembled at DESE. Mary Kent was elated. Soon Cameron Schulz would be brought to justice. That is what they all believed, but before Cameron left his home in San Francisco, he hid all incriminating evidence of his most rewarding escapades.

They now knew who he is and what he looked like. He would soon be in their hands, with the aid of other Federal Agencies. Mary Kent had the authority to arrest and detain and order all other agencies, both Federal and Civilian, to follow her commands.

Following the evidence that Cameron provided for the purchase of his air reservation, they were able to learn where he lived and authorities were upon his premises almost immediately. They stood by in surveillance waiting for Cameron to leave his abode.

When they saw him leave and determined that he would be away for a moderately long period of time, they made entry to his residence. However, they were dismayed. They were not able to find anything incriminating because Cameron had wisely hidden it all.

The reason Cameron became extra cautious was because of the lack of control he encountered with Henry. The finding of himself awakening alongside a spilled scrying bowl with a gold brick near his head which ached, made Cameron decide that matters were getting too unpredictable and became cautious. He hid all possible evidence against him. There was nothing to find.

Cameron was taken into custody upon his arrival in White Plains, NY, Westchester County Airport, HPN. Mary Kent, Jack Henigson and Henry were there. Henry was relieved that he finally met the person that had caused him, and his friends, so much grief. He knew it was now all over.

Custody was short lived, however, because there was no physical evidence reported against Cameron. He would have to be caught in the act of committing or causing the commission of a crime.

He was released.

However, prior to Mary's permitting Cameron's release, she and her closest associates quizzed Cameron extensively. Cameron did not lose his "gifts" and he knew what was at hand. He read the minds of Henry, Jack and Mary as much as he could. The minds of Henry and Jack were now next to impossible to read. Each had developed barriers against Cameron's invasions. Mary's was easy to read.

He could read that the authorities were on to him and that Mary, among others, simply wanted to "catch him in the act".

Cameron took that as a joke because he could get one of his controlled flunkies to do his bidding and be long gone before anything was noted to be missing. There could be no connection.

What Cameron is missing in his thinking is the fact that both Henry and Jack can read Cameron's mind. There is no reverse reading for Cameron because both Henry and Jack are now able to cloak their thoughts. Cameron has no idea that his thoughts are public between Jack and Henry. This is a mistake for Cameron, but both Jack and Henry know that.

## Chapter Thirty-Three

# Conceit Will Betray You

Almost immediately after Mary let Cameron go that Cameron thought of newly created plans. He obviously could not be the one to enter wealthy estate houses to seek and steal valuable gems, gold and silver as well as any cash or valuable paintings.

He knew that and sat on a bench only a block or two away from Mary's office and stayed very still with his chin down and almost touching his chest for a good half hour, just thinking on and on. He knew that he was being watched. Those were Mary's instructions to her personnel. "Follow him. See where he goes and what he does. All we need to do is to catch him 'in the act' of stealing and so forth".

Cameron knew this, as he could read Mary's not-so-secret thoughts. He knew what she was planning, and he would be conversely planning how to get around it. The question was how!

Cameron went through his mental list of "flunkies".

But unknown to Cameron was that as his mind recalled those mentally controlled "robots", that both Henry and Jack were able to "tune in" on Cameron's most secret trove of robotic individuals. Cameron's mind was an open book and both Jack and Henry and both kept notes on each and every one.

Cameron's army would soon be eliminated as DESE would make contact with each individual and make them aware of what was happening to them. They would be rescued. DESE's effective goal would be to neutralize Cameron's control over these individuals.

Cameron rose from the bench with a smug smile on his face. "I am going to outwit them all!" he thought. That thought was also mentally "overheard" by the two DESE agents monitoring Cameron.

Jack and Henry silently looked at each other and smiled. Words were not needed. "That's what he thinks!" They both thought in unison. They were not going to report what they had learned to Mary because they knew that Mary's mind was another open book to Cameron.

They were forced to keep Cameron's thoughts to themselves. If Mary knew all, Cameron would know all and then any of his plans would change. Jack and Henry wanted Cameron's plans to be changed by being caught in the act and by the authorities!

Both Jack and Henry were empowered as members of DESE as "authorities" and they would place Cameron under arrest once they had sufficient proof.

## Chapter Thirty-Four

# Polo at Conyers Farm

The day arrived. The sun was in its full glory and the sky was a beautiful clear blue with only a wisp of a cloud here and there. The charitable match was sponsored by the Greenwich Polo Club. The crowd was sizable because Prince William was to play as part of the Black Watch Team. Excitement was everywhere and the Sunday afternoon in July was sparking with palpable stimulation. It touched everyone.

Everyone but Cameron Schulz was thrilled. This was a working day for Cameron and a day he designed for very serious business. Today was the day to get his "flunkies" or "robotic" agents to do his deeds. His mentally controlled individuals each had assignments to first learn what families were at the Polo Grounds and then to find where they lived. Cameron was also at the Polo Grounds and was watching the match, but only his body was there. His eyes saw almost nothing. His mind was working three "robotic" Cameron mind-controlled agents who were now in the midst of entering unguarded houses and picking up small items such as diamonds and other gems. Cash in large bills was also taken. The entire deeds for all three flunkies took less than forty-five minutes from entry to exit.

When each of Cameron's agents left the site of theft, they were met by agents from DESE directed there by Henry and Jack Henigson. They were placed under arrest and their booty was confiscated as evidence in safe keeping sealed pouches or locked boxes.

None of this escaped Cameron. He knew that his agents were apprehended the moment that it happened. His extraordinarily well-developed mind managed all three robots at once.

In each case Cameron went into a near trance as he concentrated deeply in a quiet location near the Conyers Farm Polo Field. His near trances lasted about fifteen minutes each.

The agents took their suspects to headquarters. There they were arraigned and kept in custody pending a hearing the next day. Their booty was kept in one of the safe vaults at the Greenwich Police Department.

The next morning, just before noon, each defendant appeared before the local magistrate. Each defendant pleaded not guilty. They knew nothing of what they had done and although their bodies were present and performed the thefts, their minds were not their own. They were remotely controlled, a situation very familiar to Henry and to Walter. The charges were read and the booty was presented as evidence to the Judge to hold the criminals for trial and sentencing.

There arose one very big problem in each of the three cases. Although the evidence had been securely kept under lock and key, the evidence containers were empty. There was no evidence to present to the Judge. Without evidence of theft the charges were void and Cameron's robots were dismissed and were allowed to leave.

Cameron did not wait around to protect his robotic agents. He knew that they did not need protection. Cameron knew what his robots stole. He saw what they saw, and, as with the gold from the U.S. Treasury, he mastered the actual implementation of Einstein's theory that all solid material substances were actually in molecular motion. Each substance had its own "frequency" or rate of molecular movement which determined its very nature. Cameron simply willed the dissociation of each of the items into a transcontinental miasma. A very rich cloud containing an ionized mist of stolen items which then traveled through the air to Cameron's home in San Francisco near the Embarcadero.

Cameron was going home. He did his work as he had planned. His hands never touched any of the stolen items. He was clean.

Cameron picked up his return flight to San Francisco, SFO, at White Plains' Westchester County Airport, HPN, between Interstate 640 and New York State Route 120 near Rye Lake in short order. He had to make a connection at Chicago's O'Hare Airport, ORD. This took time. He had to wait an hour and one-half at Chicago to catch his flight to SFO.

## Chapter Thirty-Five

# SURPRISE, SURPRISE!

Henry and Jack Henigson consulted with each other, and Henry told Jack of the gold bars he saw at Cameron's lair. Jack recalled how he teleported one of the gold bricks at Cameron's head when he was once again trying to gain control of Henry's mind.

It came to the both at the very same moment. Cameron, and his super Noetic powers and embellishment of Einstein's molecular theory, had dissociated both the U.S, Treasury's gold bricks and the stolen items from Greenwich into their molecular components and mentally had them transported, most likely to his home in San Francisco. That is why there was no evidence at the arraignment of his robotic flunkies.

It did not take long for Henry to get in contact with Elizabeth Sam. One thought and she was there, or here, that is.

Henry related to Elizabeth what had happened and what both he and Jack surmised: the stolen items are now at Cameron's apartment location. It was then that Elizabeth volunteered. She would take her collar/necklace, place it on the ground and they would be off to show up inside Cameron's apartment without opening a door or breaking a window. They know where he lived as all the information was contained in his flight reservation application. They would be there instantaneously, while Cameron was making his flights of many hours returning to San Francisco.

They agreed. The collar was placed on the floor. Cameron's address, including apartment number, was dialed into the collar. All three held hands and stepped into a ring of light around the collar. The bright purplish circular light perimeter was about three feet wide.

That was all it took. Whoosh! They were at DESE headquarters one instant and within a minute or less, they were in the center of Cameron's apartment.

Henry, Elizabeth and Jack looked around the apartment. They investigated the cabinet. There were the Fort Knox gold bars. They looked throughout the kitchen and found nothing. They went through his bedroom, its night table and bureau. They again found nothing.

Henry recognized the scrying bowl from his "phantom's" adventures. It was two-thirds full of water and deep inside its base, at the bottom of the bowl, were all the stolen items.

Jack and Elizabeth cried out to Henry, "Caution". Don't touch anything.

Jack said," We have some time. Let us think this thing out. "

Both nodded their heads in agreement. They realized that there were many consequences involved in any decision they would make. Cameron presented with many unique parameters.

The three of them would make very long-lasting decisions and Cameron presented very complex facets for them. They could not communicate with Mary because their position would be immediately blown. Cameron would know all at the very same time Mary did. No, this decision had to be made privately, between the three of them, and in secret.

They were all capable of keeping their thoughts private, except as they wished between each other, but away from the possibility of interception by Cameron. He would be surprised to see DESE agents inside his locked apartment.

## Chapter Thirty-Six

# CAMERON'S FATE

The trio waited for hours before Cameron arrived. Although he possessed the ability to dissociate and tele-transport molecular, formerly solid substances, he was not able to do the same for himself. He was afraid to even try. Imagine that if he *could* dissociate himself, then who would cause him to be transported? Cameron would be a floating fog of substance without any ability to transport or restore his own body into himself!

This was a chance Cameron would not take. How would he ever re-associate his cells back into "Cameron" at the other end? No, he was fearful of even thinking about it or even trying. Thus, the long, physically tortuous transcontinental plane rides.

After about five hours of waiting, the door to Cameron's apartment was noisily unlocked and in came the master of the house, Cameron. He had only a small carry-on suitcase with only several days' wardrobe and toiletries.

He had no suspicion that uninvited guests were eagerly waiting for him.

Cameron dropped his carry-on suitcase on a chair in the hallway which was part of the entrance to the main area in his apartment. He was eager for a drink of ice-cold water and made it headlong to the automatic water/ice dispenser on his fancy refrigerator. He placed a glass in the dispenser area and after it was filled, he took it and turned about while taking a sip of the needed water.

He choked on the first swallow. There, sitting at his desk and chairs in the most special part of his apartment were three strangers, each of them keeping their silence.

Cameron spluttered, "What? Who the hell are you? What are you doing in my apartment? How did you get here? Who let you in?

Cameron's face turned red in anger and flustered at this invasion. He was indignant but after all the fluster left him, he quieted down after several minutes and waited for an answer.

His answer came quickly and with authority. Jack Henigson displayed his Federal DESE badge and I.D. Cameron was silent and his demeanor settled. "Mr. Schulz, I must place you under arrest for theft and possession of stolen items. This is only for a start. We must talk more about some very serious matters.

Jack then communicated with Walter Murphy and no sooner had the thought left his mind, a flaming, horseless chariot fitted with comfortable cushions appeared out of nowhere in a fiery flash right between the DESE trio and the apartment exit. Cameron was trapped. Cameron was shocked.

He thought to himself, "What manner of people are these who appear out of nowhere? What is happening?" Cameron was bewildered.

"Cameron, I will tell you what manner of people we are and what is happening", said Jack.

Cameron cocked an eye, raised an eyebrow and looked straight at Jack, eye to eye.

"Well?", he asked.

"We are a different variety of you, Cameron, a much different variety. We all have abilities which, like yours, are extraordinary. We are on to what you do and have been doing." Jack continued.

"Please," interjected Walter, "you have been doing this for a number of years, have you not?"

Walter displayed more than just objective observation, he displayed anger. Walter believed that here was the man who afflicted him in his youth. This has been a goal for Walter all his life. He was both angry and pleased at the same time. He said to himself, "This is the man I have been looking for all these years. Look at him. He has no life, no friends."

Walter was at a loss as to how to act or know what to do. He thought, privately and to his most inner self, the part of him which suffered from having been taken advantage of so many years ago in his defenseless youth, "What do I do now that I have the bastard?"

Cameron replied, "What are you talking about? I have no idea of what you are talking about!" This time Cameron was indignant, feigning innocence.

Jack Henigson then said, "Perhaps words will not clear up the matter."

Jack turned towards his companions and said, "Mr. Schulz, I want to have a short conference with my friends. Give me a moment and I think I can make everything quite clear to you."

CHAPTER THIRTY-SEVEN

# CLARIFICATION

Cameron was left alone while the foursome moved away to a more private area in the apartment. Despite Cameron's ability to read and overhear thoughts, he was at a loss. Each of the foursome were able to fully cloak their thoughts. There was no sound whatsoever. Their conversation was not only secret but silent. It was mind to mind, thought to thought.

There were motions and hand waving but no sound, no word. Ultimately, there was agreement and a "yes" was the obvious result. They were all in agreement. Cameron was wary. He knew agreement most likely spelled an undesirable response. Only Cameron knew everything he ever did or ever caused. He willed himself not to recall all his past deeds because he knew that the foursome would be able to read his mind and they would know all his deeds. Cameron made his mind a blank sheet.

The group returned to Cameron's immediate area and stopped. No one said a word and just stood there looking at Cameron. Elizabeth mentally communicated with Jack and thought "Jack, you start. Let him know of our decision."

Jack stepped forward. "Mr. Schultz," he started. "It is rare indeed that we find an individual with your abilities who uses them for their own selfish greed. I don't know if you are aware, but you are not the only one with these abilities. There are many of us."

Walter chimed in, "Schultz, it's like this. I have a very strong inkling that you were the one who caused me much in the way of misery and guilt in my youth. I find that it is both hard to forgive and to forget. Right now, I'd like to beat the bejeepers out of you and it's very hard for me to resist punching you in the nose!"

Walter's anger was very easy to sense, and Schultz stepped back and away from the threat.

Seemore now put in his two cents. "Talking about noses, mine is unique, don't you agree Cameron?"

Being called by his first name was a shocker for Cameron. He has not heard his name spoken for many years. It was especially shocking for him to be in the presence of a real gnome with a bright red nose. He was not even sure that such creatures existed!

Seemore went on, "Cameron, you are most likely only aware of a small part of who and what you are. If you only knew earlier in your life you may have taken a different path and have done some good in the world besides simply feeding your greed, because that is what you have done."

"You are greedy and you have nothing around you but material things. There is no love, no warmth, no affection; you are one miserable excuse for a human being. It makes me glad to be a gnome. Just look around. There is nothing but material things and things you possess by taking advantage of the innocent, like Walter and like our Henry. Shame on you Cameron, Shame, Shame, Shame!

Cameron looked down on this small creature compared to him. He was shocked that this thing from fairy-tale land was here to give him the dickens. He could not respond.

Elizabeth Sam just sat in silence, at least to a degree. She decided that she would also interrogate Cameron, but differently from her companions, just to learn something more about Cameron's communicative abilities.

"Cameron," she started, "Look at your scrying bucket. Nothing is there!"

Cameron instantly sat up, head erect and looked towards his scrying bowl. He rapidly got up off his seat and rapidly ran towards the bowl. Elizabeth Sam just proved and learned two things about Cameron.

Cameron could receive mental telepathy and also that he did not know from where it came. His thievery was also proved because he did expect to see the gems and other precious items at the bottom of the bowl.

Not one of the DESE group disturbed anything. That was one of the immediate orders Jack Henigson strictly gave upon their arrival. Nothing was to be disturbed because it consisted of a chain of evidence. Cameron's run towards the bowl was the absolute clincher.

Cameron gave a sigh of relief that his items had arrived, but his relief changed rapidly to "Oh doggone! I just showed them that I am guilty of the crimes of which they are accusing me."

He went back to his seat and sat silently. He waited for the next thing, whatever it was, to happen to him.

That next thing happened immediately. Jack rose and approached Cameron, face to face.

"Cameron, we are federal agents and have the authority to place you under arrest."

Cameron became very serious and sober and silent.

Jack continued, "However you present both unique problems and opportunity. Considering that, I think we need to transport you back to our headquarters and simply detain you for in depth interrogation and investigation."

Cameron shuddered, not because he was being arrested, but more so because he was exhausted from his long airplane ride. He did not feel he would be up to an immediate return trip.

Cameron protested and begged, "I just got off the plane. The trip was long. I had to make connections after waiting a long time for each of my connection planes to arrive. Please let me rest a while."

Jack responded, "You won't need a rest. We will be at headquarters in a few moments."

Cameron looked puzzled. "Indeed? A few moments? How could he do that?" After all, it took Cameron hours to fly back to San Francisco. It had to be impossible to be in Washington in a "few moments"!

Jack stood Cameron up, had him placed his hands behind his back and handcuffed him.

Then all, except Walter, stood in a circle, holding hands about Elizabeth Sam's communication "collar". Jack held onto Cameron on one side and Seemore held onto him on the other side. Cameron was bewildered.

"What kind of game is this?" Cameron protested.

Jack, the authority figure, answered, "This is no game. This is serious business. Just hold tight."

As those words were spoken, Elizabeth triggered the return button and instantly the group found themselves cross country and in the confines of DESE headquarters. Shortly after their arrival, Walter flashed onto the scene again in his flaming chariot! Cameron just about fell over in shock!

Although Cameron was "gifted" he had no inkling that such persons as these ever existed! Everything was either shocking or at least a surprise. A trip which took Cameron many hours of flying and connection time was made in the matter of a moment or two. "How did they do that?" he wondered to himself.

## Chapter Thirty-Eight

# CAMERON'S INTERROGATION

Jack Henigson wasted no time questioning Cameron. He began. "Cameron, you have shown some remarkable talents. We all want to go over each one of them in detail.

The last words: "in detail" were stressed and Cameron took notice that they had a very serious connotation to them.

Jack continued, "How did you transport those three gold bricks in your cabinet from the U.S. Treasury to your possession? The Treasury is heavily guarded, and the barriers are insurmountable by just about every living thing. How did you do that?"

Cameron stood in silence. He did not move, flinch or even change his poker player facial expression.

Henigson went on, "How did you get the "robotic agents" in your control to send you the gems and precious items now resting in your San Francisco scrying bowl?"

Without waiting for a reply, Jack continued, "Furthermore, how did you get to control those "robotic victims" to do your bidding and cooperate with you in criminal activity?"

Jack was on the run.

Cameron could have been made of stone. Jack knew that he would have to find a chink in this man's "armor". The question is what would that be? Cameron was a loner. He had no friends or family. He had no pets. He had nothing to lose except his possessions.

Jack reasoned that he would have to find something that was most precious to him but could think of nothing.

Elizabeth Sam noted his quandary and went to his side. No one knew how adept at reading mental telepathy Cameron was. Each DESE member present was afraid to do much "thinking" as it were.

Elizabeth Sam and the rest of the group were now very accomplished at the "double thought" transmission technique which proved very effective in preventing being "overheard" by outsiders, including Cameron.

Elizabeth, partially vocally and partially mentally, had a short conversation with Jack in his onslaught against Cameron.

"Very simple." She thought transferred to Jack. "He can control the actions of other 'gifteds' and I would bet that the entire process can be turned against him. After all, look at what Henry did in resisting Cameron's efforts to control him."

Jack's ears perked up. "Of course! That must be the 'chink' in this stone man's armor!" Jack asked himself and Elizabeth, "But how can we do it?"

Elizabeth responded half and half telepathically and orally to further confuse anything that Cameron might be able to understand, "First let us get him away from all of us and place him in one of our specially guarded, very comfortable cells and lock him up."

Jack replied quizzically, "No, he would just teleport the keys to the cell to his possession and escape."

"Not if we use the keys that we use to lock up the time capsule photographs. They are enchanted and not opened except by special codes. You recall that should unauthorized persons attempt to open them that they would release the lock, bark, drop to the floor and chase and bite who ever attempts to do so." Elizabeth responded. "Cameron would get the scare of his life and not dare re-attempt escape!"

"Good idea", Jack was delighted in this Eureka moment.

The group were all double think informed of the result and reasoning to have Cameron removed to a thought transfer proof cell and away from all.

## Chapter Thirty-Nine

# SOLITUDE AND SILENT CONTEMPLATION

It came to pass. Cameron timidly accepted his fate, and he was led to the thought proof and telepathy resistant lockup.

It was remarkably well outfitted with a sofa as well as a bed and nicely lit. There was no entertainment center, phone or radio. In that sense it was sparse. Otherwise, it was possibly even a bit more comfortable than Cameron's own quasi-wizard's home!

Cameron had much to think about: namely, how did he arrive at this location at this time in his life, nearly middle-aged. He felt he had much soul searching to do. This was not where someone with his abilities should ever be. He wondered, "What happened?"

Cameron thought back and then he thought back some more. He asked himself, "Was it the last time he tried to control that new young robot by the name of Henry. Henry was the only robot who resisted Cameron's efforts. That had to be it."

Cameron stopped his attempts to control Henry.

He thought aloud, "But I wonder if I had continued in my effort to control him, could I have been successful?" He then added, "Probably not!"

This was a question Cameron could never get answered. This was when Cameron arranged for his "robots" to enter unprotected houses of the very wealthy in Greenwich, CT. It was during this time that the Prince of Wales engaged in a charitable benefit at the Conyers Farm Polo Field. Henry was to be one of his choice robots for the purpose, but Cameron failed in enlisting him.

"That has to be it!" said Cameron in his Eureka moment. "Henry is a DESE agent. The entire DESE organization had to have been watching me via Henry and my every effort to engage my "robot" army as well as my every movement!"

Cameron was now very satisfied with his conclusions, which happened to be 100% correct.

He asked himself, "Now what? What happens now? Am I going to prison or what?"

Cameron guessed that such would be his fate and no other.

Then he reasoned, "But this is no ordinary jail and this is no ordinary government agency. It is what it is and only the passage of time will reveal my fate."

Resigned to whatever was to come, which for once was now beyond his control, he sat back on his bunk and put his mind and himself to sleep. He could do no more.

## Chapter Forty

# RESOLUTION

The DESE team brainstormed possible decisions regarding the biggest current problem on their agenda: Cameron's fate.

The main movers of the DESE organization were included in all discussions regarding Cameron. Seemore the Gnome, the trans-universe travelers Mr. Xilx and Elizabeth, Jack Henigson, Mary Kent and, of course, Henry Wilson along with the hard worker Wyatt.

Each had different versions of how to deal with Cameron from simply keeping him in a mental transfer proof prison for life to retrain his mind so that society could find a benefit in whatever services he might be able to provide.

Each recognized that Cameron had "gifts" that none of the others achieved either separately or even as a group. Each saw that Cameron was "special" and in a way that could not be ignored.

The "Nonlocality" question was "Now what?" much like Cameron's question. Einstein to the rescue! Cameron is in a thought-proof, telepathic proof cell. His question of "Now what?" had to have been delivered via nonlocality, not mental telepathy or thought transfer. In a sense it was coincidental or was it? Ask Einstein.

Nevertheless, the similar question existed and it was "*solution-time*".

Seemore was the most severe and said in a half humor, half serious "let's roast him for dinner!" His red face became redder and his nose almost glowed. Of course he was not serious, but very frustrated and that answer signified the level of a hard-to-reach resolution.

Next came Jack Henigson's statement that "Cameron was simply a wayward child because of all the items he sought, and stole had really no significance to him or his welfare."

Mary Kent tended to agree with Jack. "After all, we really know nothing of Cameron: Where did he grow up and under what circumstances. How did his fantastic abilities develop? We need to know more about this man."

Mr. Xilx simply said, "This man has nothing and wants nothing, except to control others. Look around and recall what we saw at his apartment. There was nothing there of any personal significance, nothing of any personal warmth."

Elizabeth agreed with Mr. Xilx and added, "Perhaps we need to investigate his past before we come to any conclusions."

Henry simply nodded in agreement.

Suddenly there was a "whoosh" and Walter appeared in his usual chariot.

"Hold on there!" he exclaimed as he jumped out of his disappearing vehicle. "I was the one most affected by this man! You should have included me in any decision regarding Cameron's fate!" Walter was quite obviously upset that he was not invited to this session.

Everyone in the group was taken aback. Of course they should have included Walter! In unison they all said, "We're very sorry, Walter. It was simply an oversight which should never have occurred."

Henry had the gumption to ask the barely composed arrival, "Walter, what do you think should be done, or really ***could*** be done with Cameron? His powers and abilities are more extreme than those with which most of us here can cope."

Now it was Walter's turn to be taken aback while the others in the group were still smarting from Walter's scolding.

Walter never expected that this question would ever be handed to him in apparent retaliation for his criticism. Nevertheless, there it was. "What would **I** do with Cameron? Why I would, I would, I would " The thought trailed on into oblivion.

Walter could not answer the question as much as he wished he could. He knew Schulz was the enemy of his youth. He was waiting for this moment. But the moment was here. But the retribution, the anger, the vengeance Walter earlier experienced had faded. Walter was now confounded by the word "reason".

The solution for Cameron's crimes has to take on the challenge of Cameron's unique abilities. He could escape from any ordinary prison.

Walter thought, "Perhaps we **do** need to know more of Cameron. There has to be a way for us to enter into his past and to determine what made him this way. Why did these "gifts" develop?"

His thoughts were communal. Each member of the group heard and understood. Walter's thoughts were "broadcast" to group members and reflected the sum conclusions of the group members.

He added and communicated the confounding question to each member: "But how can we enter into his mind and read his past experiences?"

## CHAPTER FORTY-ONE

# MARY KENT

**M**ary Kent was not aware of any of these mental communications, not being one of the "gifted". Mental telepathy was something she was aware of but not capable of performing. The others could read her thoughts, although she had taken lessons in "double think", she was still a novice.

The group knew that she was being left out, and as a result, informed her vocally of their thoughts and conclusions: "We have to enter into Cameron's brain and learn about his past and whatever made him as he is today."

It did not take Mary long to come up with an answer. DESE has advanced incredible mind and mood reading surreptitious equipment and Mary would make it available. The best part was that there had to be no physical connection to Cameron's body or brain. The fancy DESE equipment only had to be in proximity to Cameron and all his life's story would soon be community knowledge.

The DESE device was the "**<u>Thought Reader and Inducer</u>**" and is used as when the DESE previously had to combat the evil witches. The "**TRI**" for short, could read the thoughts of those persons of interest and even induce pre-coded thoughts into their minds. This came in the form of a fountain pen called the "**<u>Cogito Lector</u>**".

This item would be vocally triggered by the owner's voice frequency and the command "**cogito**" to induce thoughts and set the "**lecto**" switch to read Cameron's memory, both conscious and subconscious to his early youth. All visual and non-visual memories, thoughts and more would be stored within the "Lector" or reader as it may be more accurately described.

The group became delightfully excited just like children! They had a method to enter into Cameron's past and they could even record it for later playback! Mary revealed that she "just happened" to have had a Cogito-Lector in her handbag. She presented it to the group, each member of which were now suspiciously pleased because each wondered if Mary had used the instrument against them. Nevertheless, there was sort of a carnival atmosphere as all members of the group silently followed Mary down to Cameron's holding cell.

Silently, they positioned the Cogito-Lector, turned it on and Mary whispered "LECTO" and the machine began to record Cameron's memory. Mary set the remote feature on it and tuned into her receiver and all left Cameron's immediate vicinity to "listen in" from some distance from where Cameron was resting.

# Chapter Forty-Two

# TUNING IN

Cameron was very relaxed and bored. He made his mind a blank. He was in despair because there was nothing he could do but relax and relax he did, sort of.

The result was as if he were in quasi-hypnosis, self-induced and next to dozing off. His mind was wide open and defenseless. The Lecto had full access to Cameron's memory, including memories of his childhood.

The DESE group learned that Cameron's youth was not easy and that he sometimes had very little to eat and even had a hard time finding something decent to wear. It was only by accident that Cameron discovered his extraordinary abilities.

His aunt Matilda, took as good care of him as she could after he was orphaned at twelve years of age as a result of the Spanish train wreck that took the lives of his mother and father. The DESE organization looked into the history of his parents and discovered that they were both "gifted" and thus they accounted for Cameron's abilities.

Cameron was without guidance as a child. His poor aunt Matilda was not gifted and was not ever aware of Cameron's talents. Cameron grew up without knowledge of his inherited gifts and without guidance he took the easy, but illegal, path.

The DESE members all agreed that these most likely were the reasons for Cameron's wayward behavior. Poverty, the need for food and life's basics, funding, education et cetera were denied him. Cameron was next to living on the street. He had no choice. Cameron had to rely on himself or do without many of the things, possessions and sundries that make life worth living.

They also understood that he tended to be bitter over what life had unfairly dealt him and they also took note of his desire to succeed. One discovery like the coins in the magic shop and the traffic lights led to one discovery and another and another.

Ultimately, Cameron was able to control the "robots", other gifteds, with less ability to resist commands from Cameron. This resulted in thefts and permitted Cameron a lifestyle improvement.

After Aunt Matilda passed away, he was totally on his own and had to provide for himself, which he did the best way he knew. That way was to use his powers to obtain his needs whether it was money or material things. He entered the lives of Walter Murphy and Henry Wilson, both in their unprotected and unwise youth, and made them his unknowing agents. Cameron ultimately gave up on both.

Cameron never met either one of them, or any of his other "robots". He did not need to. He did not know any of them, until now. He gathered their thoughts from the ether of space because none of them had the ability to "cloak" their thoughts. Cameron simply "plugged in" his own commands and they obeyed. Cameron had no idea that his commands would ever be met. He was surprised when they were obeyed. It was never required that he meet them. All that was required was that the robot-like actions of his "agents" would ultimately get their ill-gotten gains to him and that is what he lived on.

That was until Walter and then Henry put up resistance. This was when his "reign" began to collapse, although Cameron had no idea that the end was near. The signals were obvious.

The end was here. Now he was DESE's problem because he could never be held in any jail or by any restraint whatsoever. The members of DESE had a tough nut to crack and that was "what to do with Cameron". They were back to square one, but now they had knowledge and that knowledge gave them power.

Each one had to question how this man who could atomize gold in the U.S. Treasury and transport the molecular particles three thousand miles away. He felt it was ironic that he had to take an airplane from White Plains airport to San Francisco. It sounds like a contradiction, and each felt that it would only be a matter of time before this near genius criminal would be able to transport himself through space and distance as he did with other material things.

They wondered that "Either he does not know how or he is afraid to do that with his body."

The fact that he was able to "dissociate" inanimate object's molecules and transmit them through space only to be reassembled later at the desired destination using only his willpower made him fearful of doing the same to his own body! He had to question and wonder if, how and who would put his own de atomized molecular body back together! The fear that his own body would remain in molecular space and never be reassembled precluded any attempt at his doing so!

The question was what to do with that knowledge and power!

# PROPOSITION

The close knit DESE notables put their literal "heads" together and achieved a common thought which they fed to Mary. Mary would think that the ideas she came up with were her own. That was the main idea. The "gifteds" essentially spoon fed her ideas, but they were the communal thought of the entire group, Mary's induced ideas would be energetically encouraged, praised and agreed upon as being ideal. Mary would believe that the ideas she proposed were of her own making and she was self-impressed with how bright she was. Quite self-satisfied indeed!

"My dear friends", she started, "Since it is not possible to restrain Cameron in an ordinary cell or prison, it is a task we should not even attempt to do so. He is instead in an enchanted cell which has devices in it and around it to prevent Cameron from using any of his powers, mental or physical.

Let us see if we can re-educate and show him all that he has been missing over the years. Cameron did not even know that people like him existed until now! He was lonely and alone in the world with no one to whom to turn."

The group all agreed. After all, the thoughts which emanated from Mary's mouth gave voice to their own collective ideas, but they gave Mary the credit!

"I suggest that we keep him in lockup for a while. Just so that Cameron gets time to reflect on simply nothing, nothing to do or accomplish. Since his powers are ineffective in his cell, Cameron truly will get what he needs, namely 'time off' from the ambitions of his former life."

Mary continued, "What Cameron needs is friendship and counsel. He needs to know that he is not alone and that there are others, though not many, like him and with "gifts" like his. He needs to be shown how those special gifts can be used for the betterment of mankind and the world. He has never had any friends or acquaintances which were his mental equal to show him the way. He always felt superior to those about him, and he was.

That is not the way it is now. Cameron is in for a very big change, and it is a change which we all will supply, slowly and one at a time. I am sure that it will also be a big surprise to him as well."

## Chapter Forty-Four

# SLOW AND STEADY WINS THE RACE

Mary suggested that the assault on Cameron's mental state and his crooked, criminal ambitions would be "gentle persuasion". That persuasion would not come from one of the active members of DESE, but rather one of its agents group, the Wispy Whisperers. Seemore Manlein, now a very active DESE member, would contact them on behalf of DESE.

The idea is that the Wispy Whisperers would be apprised of what DESE's goal is in relation to Cameron and then would essentially feed him ideas to the good and away from evil and criminal activity. That would only be the start of change for Cameron.

One by one, each of the DESE members would separately enter Cameron's cell and converse with him and give him counsel. Since each of the DESE members that were allowed to enter into Cameron's cell were now well educated in "double-think" and cloaking their thoughts, Cameron would not be able to influence their minds, firstly because he could not read their minds, and secondly because those agents that were allowed to enter the cell were trained to resist and repel all of Cameron's influences.

For Cameron it was like hitting a brick wall. The only possible result would be for Cameron to listen, pay attention again and again and again. Agent consultation and Wispy Whisper influence would be effective on their own. Cameron did not have a chance to resist. In this case, Cameron was the one being influenced and without his even being aware that he was changing.

Nevertheless, DESE would not take any chances. DESE equipment also included mind and mood reading equipment in the Cogito-Lector. All agreed that it would be used to monitor Cameron's mental state and thoughts and to additionally "feed" his mind and memory with beneficial thoughts. Cameron's ideas would be an open book to DESE.

Nothing would be hidden.

The first member of DESE to enter Cameron's cell would be Seemore, the Gnome. The sight of Seemore alone would put Cameron's mind into neutral. Cameron would not know how to deal with a Gnome. "After all," Cameron thought, "What kind of DESE agent could this creature be anyway? What would he have to speak about with me?"

Seemore responded, having read Cameron's mind, "I am a very special type of 'creature', as it were. I am from all over the world. I am not a human and yet I am human. I am spirit just as your thoughts are spirit. I am old and I am wise. My life span is over one thousand of your years. You will go and I will still be here. So, listen to my guidance and take my advice, only if you are smart."

"We, all the members of DESE and more, are fully aware of everything in your past. We know all that you have done, mostly illegally. You are in very serious trouble." Seemore continued.

Cameron flinched. "How could they know of my past? How could they know what I have done? What does this pipsqueak know about putting me into 'serious trouble'?"

Seemore continued, "I know you have doubts and question our abilities to know all that I have just stated. Trust me. There is more to DESE and its members than you will ever assimilate or ever discover."

Cameron sat in silent attention. The Wispy Whisperers already had planted the thought in Cameron's head that he needed to reform and respect the members of DESE. They essentially put fear into his mind, a fear which would not easily go away and one he respected. Accountability for his past deeds and thoughts was not something Cameron ever suspected he would ever have to face. But there it was: Accountability.

Seemore continued his lecture; "Thievery and mental control of the naïve "gifted" person is something which is criminal and never permitted. You essentially made these people into your zombie-like robotic slaves. You are accountable for that as well as their deeds. You could be in prison for many decades, if not for life."

Cameron bowed his head and humbly said, "I'm sorry. I had to survive. I had nowhere to live, nothing to wear, nothing to eat. I had no choice. I am so very sorry."

Seemore answered, "I am glad to hear that. Perhaps there is hope for you. I am going to leave now. Another agent will be speaking with you. I suggest that you pay heed to what they have to say to you."

Seemore left.

One by one, each of the elected DESE members entered Cameron's cell. Each gave Cameron a similar tongue lashing. Cameron was humble and crushed. He never expected to be lambasted because of his "gifts". Cameron believed that he was just like everyone else on earth but just "happened" to be able to control those people and things around him. He never realized that he was one of the "gifted".

He was not able to control everything, but just ***nearly*** everything. That inability led him to think he was normal and when control happened, that he was just "lucky". Cameron had no idea that he was different and that he was "special" among human beings.

The Wispy Whisperers continued their work, both day and night. It made no difference whether Cameron was awake or asleep. The Whisperers kept on, supplementing the efforts of DESE members.

Cameron had no chance. Change was the only way Cameron could ever put his mind to peace. At night he sleeplessly tossed and turned. During the day he developed acid indigestion. He was unendingly aggravated and worried.

One night, when he was sound asleep, he shouted out, "O.K! O.K! I'll be good. I'll change! I'll change! I'll change!"

## CHAPTER FORTY-FIVE

# COGITO-LECTOR

Cameron's shout was so loud that all the DESE residents heard it either directly or mental telepathically. Those who were asleep were awakened. Each wondered what was happening. It was a very loud, earth-shaking, bed-shaking event!

All gathered in the meeting room to understand what had happened. Each asked the other and all came up with "I don't know. There was this sudden loud noise. I thought the building was disintegrating or an earthquake."

This time it was the more "ordinary" and ungifted Mary who came up with the answer.

"It is the Cogito-Lector which sets off our alarm. It awakened us all. The Cogito showed that Cameron 'broke' and is on his way to rehabilitation." Mary explained to all in a matter-of-fact manner, without emotion, and just simply reporting to all.

The group went down to sneak a peek at Cameron's cell. He was sound asleep. This time it was a peaceful sleep. Cameron had reformed, although in his subconscious mind. He was not aware of his change, but the DESE team was. The old, criminal, thieving Cameron was no more.

Mary motioned to all to retreat away from Cameron's cell in silence so as not to disturb the newly rehabilitated Cameron. "Let him sleep in peace. Let all the work DESE and the Wispy Whisperers did sink into his brain, mind and change his spirit. Let the seed grow and change Cameron into a more civil human being, one who is of benefit to his fellow man and to society. We will check out the Cogito in the morning." Mary stated authoritatively.

# THE STATE OF CLEAR

The morning sun rose in a clear, deep blue sky. The air was crisp and invigorating.

Cameron rose from his bunk, stretched and yawned. He felt like a new man for some reason. He hadn't felt this good in a very long time. Suddenly all the worries and fears he had been harboring left him. All that was left was goodness and light.

Somehow all the cobwebs in his mind were gone. Everything was clear to him now. He realized that the DESE organization was not going to torture or imprison him. Cameron felt freedom from the past and all that had tied his mind into a knot.

He looked forward to the new day.

The Wispy Whisperers reported the success of their mission to Mary Kent and Mary spread the word to all DESE members.

The reading of the Cogito confirmed success. "The former, wicked Cameron is no more!" Mary exclaimed in her report to the DESE members which gathered about the Cogito.

Then suddenly, Mary's face blanked. All noticed it and wondered why.

The answer came quickly. The puzzled Mary asked of her fellows, "Now what do we do with Cameron?"

That was the million-dollar question. More blank faces joined Mary's.

Jack Henigson said, "We must see how rehabilitated he really is. We will have to let him out of his cell, under guard of course, and observe him. We can further introduce him to his other "gifted" fellow members of DESE. All DESE members have to be wary of any attempt by Cameron to mind control them and report it immediately if they have the slightest sense of any attempt by him to do so.

Mr. Xilx added, "There is both danger and opportunity here. As Cameron gets to know us, he might find weaknesses among us and take advantage. On the other hand, we can learn from Cameron those gifts that we do not have. For instance, how did he dissociate the Fort Knox gold into air and get it to San Francisco?"

"We have to be aware of both opportunity and risk here." Mr. Xilx concluded.

And so it began: the integration of criminal Cameron into Citizen Cameron, a very interesting adventure!

## Chapter Forty-Seven

# CITIZEN CAMERON

Cameron was very surprised when all members of the elite DESE delegation came to his cell to invite him to join them at breakfast. Cameron was further amazed that the group breakfast was held <u>outside</u> his cell and in the dining hall as well. This was as much a shock to him as was his surprise capture in San Francisco.

This was the result of the earlier DESE meeting, with all their heads and thoughts together and all options considered.

Basically, it was concluded that lifetime confinement in telepathic resistant jails, there really was no way to control deeds of a near-wizard, Cameron.

Lifetime confinement was overkill, and not necessary, especially after the history of Cameron's youth, his trials and tribulations came to light. In any case, it was believed that eventually Cameron would escape the security of confinement mentally for certain and even physically as well. The only logical defense would be to cause Cameron to reform into a decent and responsible citizen, and hopefully that is what they would achieve.

No. It was decided that Cameron would become the "model" citizen, especially in the eyes of DESE. Should Cameron achieve that goal, he would be the "model" and decent citizen they all believed he could be once shown a viable alternative to his past.

The breakfast was excellent, and Cameron made the best of it. He was starving, both for good peerage company and really good food not served in solitary.

It was Mr. Xilx, the alien in a dignified senior human form who started the conversation and led Cameron into discussion. Each member of the DESE team could now cloak their thoughts, but Cameron's mind was a open book to them. His thoughts were immediately known to each DESE attendee.

"Cameron", Xilx started with extending a warm fatherly arm about Cameron's shoulder, "We have looked into your history and we feel that you require the equivalent of 're-education' and to be shown a more rewarding lifestyle. Such a lifestyle is one which would keep you in contact with persons who are your equals and with whom you can honestly communicate and learn."

Cameron had enough of Wispy Whisperers and thoughts of "goodness" fed into his nightly dreams. He already declared that he'd reform, both in his sleep and after awakening. "This may be exactly what I've been hoping for" he thought.

Xilx went on, "Cameron, you are one of the very few 'gifted' people on earth. We consider ourselves a very special group capable of doing good things for the people of the world and society at large. Our gifts are unique as are yours. We all do not posses the same abilities as the next member of our group but each supplement the other. Together we do great things."

Cameron now stood in silent wonder and looked at the very dignified Mr. Xilx. He understood every word. He asked himself "Where is this heading?"

Although Cameron felt he was secure in his thinking, his thoughts were immediately read by everyone in the group, except for Mary, the director who was not one of the so-called "gifted" and lacked certain abilities.

"Perhaps you are wondering where this conversation is going?" Without waiting for a response from Cameron whose mouth just opened to an interrupted reply, Xilx went on."

"Cameron, after reviewing your past and knowing your very unique abilities, we wonder if you would rather be a collaborative member of our group instead of an imprisoned enemy and criminal?"

Xilx stopped talking, still looking an uncomfortable Cameron directly in the eye, from eye to eye.

Cameron stared back. His shock was obvious. This was not what he expected, but better. He thought, "I can still be myself, but this time in the service of others! This is shocking! I will be with my 'contemporaries'. These are people that have similar gifts as I. I have finally found something like a 'family'. Better yet, I will have a job working for the government of all things! Who could have believed it?"

Of course, every DESE member read his thoughts and all were pleased, but there was no "yes" or "no" yet. Each one waited, expectantly hopeful.

It took Cameron only a few silent moments to recover. His answer was a resounding "Yes. Of course I would. I would consider it an honor and an opportunity that I would appreciate more than you could ever know! Yes! Yes! Yes!"

Cameron's enthusiastic answer echoed in the hall. Every DESE member was delighted in it. It was what each had hoped for, and because they could read Cameron's mind, they knew that his response and his feelings were genuine. They were all very happy.

They each now welcomed "Citizen Cameron" one by one. Cameron finally had a real home for a change. The last real home he had was with Aunt Matilda so very many years ago after which he was virtually a street urchin. He was finally happy and it showed on his face

## Chapter Forty-Eight

# INTEGRATION AND THE NEXT ADVENTURE

It was done. The mysterious disappearance of gold from Fort Knox and the sizeable thefts around the world were solved.

Cameron would not be imprisoned because no prison could ever hold him. The treatment he received at DESE rehabilitated him to a new life and a new citizenship. Prosecution was obviated. After all, who in the world was ever treated with Wispy Whisperers and Cogito-Lectors? The answer is "no one" until now, that is. The therapy was one hundred percent effective. One had to realize that Cameron's mood and his every thought was monitored. This is not ordinary "therapy" and Cameron was not an "ordinary" individual. Thus, Cameron received extraordinary attention.

Fortunately, or unfortunately, neither Cameron nor DESE would ever be the same again. Walter Murphy sought and, to his surprise, was now an associate of his former tormentor as was Henry Wilson whose resistance, with Walter Murphy's help, brought down this unintentional "criminal".

It was a happy occasion.

Henry and Elizabeth once again joined hands while smiling at each other as they left DESE headquarters happily skipping away.

Jack Henigson and Mr. Xilx took Cameron by the hand and led him on a tour of their offices and then Xilx took him home with Jack because Cameron's San Francisco home and all his possessions were confiscated by the government. Cameron's old residence was gone. It was also recognized that Cameron would need watching and further guidance.

Cameron now had a new residence with Jack and Mr. Xilx. They did not fully realize that they now had a new "buddy", one who would continue to learn and continue to be surprised.

Cameron would be taught and learn new things. Jack, Mr. Xilx and DESE would conversely be taught by Cameron and all would learn from the other. It would be an adventure yet to be told.

He still had to learn the truth about Mr. Xilx and Elizabeth Sam, didn't he? He would have great interest in learning that they are really from out of this world.

## Chapter Forty-Nine

# THE MOUTH OF TRUTH

Cameron Schultz just "squeaked by" gaining acceptance by the "elite," older and more experienced members of the U.S. Department of Extraordinary Situations and Events. Cameron is still suspect and the Henigson house serves as a "half-way" house where he can be watched and further evaluated. Half-way because of the degree to which his powers remain unknown and somewhat feared. At this point Cameron's "trust" is both guarded and uncertain, but the prospect is improving.

All alone in his room at Henigson's and Mr. Xilx's house, the in-limbo, quasi black sheep of DESE, Cameron peacefully and calmly lay there, in the sunset early evening hours, on his bed simply just staring at the blank ceiling. Aside from creating disturbance and mischief there were no distractions, books, or magazines. Still, Cameron remained content. All was well with the world and Cameron was comfy, both physically, and mentally. He said to himself, "Finally I'm at peace and

I feel safe. I'm at rest. I'm happy for a change." He then took a deep, cleansing breath.

For this emotionally unsettled soul these are remarkable thoughts. Cameron realized this as a fact indeed. The sun had set, and the almost cloudless sky held onto its extra bright full moon and Cameron was "spacing out" thinking randomly about this and that, nothing really. The window was open and screenless at this time of year because the colder weather had killed off all disturbing, biting, flying, uninvited insects. Removing the screen let the fresh air flow freely into Cameron's room.

Except for the brightness of the moon, his room would have been as dark as pitch. The moonlight still barely invaded Cameron's bedroom. It was almost impossible to see one's hand in front of one's face.

Cameron just lay on the unmade bed not even moving a muscle, not even a twitch, and silently, foolishly letting his mind wander as he allowed his point of casual concentration to remain focused on one, almost impossible to see, spot on the ceiling. As he focused on it, he would swear it was growing and he could feel that it was unrealistically "coming to life".

Cameron, the newbie to DESE, and a man who could not be restrained because of his special ability to convert material objects into their molecular components and cause their matter to virtually disintegrate and disappear, thus removing their ability to neither restrain nor contain him. Such restraints had no effect on Cameron.

"What is that "growing" ceiling spot? Why is it 'growing?'" Cameron mused. Its tendency to change to a gaping opening kept Cameron both puzzled and wary.

There was no damage to the ceiling beforehand. Although concerned, he kept his calm but ever anxious feelings to himself, mostly out of fear that either Jack Henigson or Mr. Xilx might read his mental thoughts and feelings.

He said to himself, at the risk of indiscriminately mentally telepathing his words, his thoughts. Those transmitted thoughts could be an unwanted invitation that Xilx or Henigson or both could come into his room. That was something Cameron wanted to avoid at least until the supposed "growing spot" either ceased its growth or could otherwise be explained.

Cameron was a curious being. Although Cameron possessed extraordinary powers, he was still human and such uncontrollable thoughts and feelings came into his head simply as a biological phenomenon for any human. Thoughts never stop flowering. The living mind constantly generates new thoughts on its own. Cameron feared that if his room was "invaded" by his hosts that the "spot" might stop its expansion and he would never find an explanation.

Cameron was in denial of what he saw. The spot grew as a gaping circle. There was nothing to see inside it. It strangely appeared as if there were no "inside" at all. It appeared as just a well-defined, flat, wide ring growing slowly but steadily. Cameron was beginning to be more and more concerned. He thought, hopefully privately to himself in a house where uncloaked thought telepathy was monitored by its "gifted" residents, "This is not coming from me. I am not producing this thing, whatever it is." Slowly increasing, its diameter was six inches, then ten inches. It keeps growing!"

Cameron, being the cool soul, he learned to become over his short lifetime, did not panic, nor did he ever intend or allow himself to permit the luxury of self-indulgence to that irrational emotion. "No, I don't want to disturb Jim or Mr. Xilx. I don't want them to come in here if I am not going to be devoured. But is this a "thing" or what? What the devil is this?"

Uncharacteristically, Cameron's curiosity turned into concern. Suddenly, instead of just being a flat hole, it started to develop inside space, like a mouth. Deep, dark, and black space. For effect, it now added low, deep groaning sounds, and a tongue! It was seeing teeth which quadrupled his adrenaline and cortisol levels and motivation for a Cameron solo marathon run!

He also developed the fear that his trust in DESE may have been misplaced. Perhaps because they realize they can't contain me they may see me as a danger and have conjured up this creature to simply consume me because they are afraid of me. Now instead I am afraid of what and why this thing is.

Cameron speculated, "This thing could actually swallow me!" Concern grew into apprehension. Apprehension grew into fear.

Cameron said to himself aloud, "No, I can't let this groaning thing make me panic, but I'm ready to run." Cameron subconsciously was afraid that this mysterious thing would devour and swallow him up into non-existence. He had one leg off the bed.

At that point, the open circle let out something like a yawning sound and spat out a saliva, mucous dripping flask, almost striking his head.

Cameron mused, "I guess its aim was bad," and gave out a short laugh. The wide-open circle of a mouth then quickly and loudly snapped shut like a mousetrap and disappeared, including all traces of teeth, mouth and tongue and groaning sounds, leaving only a very small dot on the ceiling where it originated. Cameron would never again trust innocence to that dot. He recognized that almost invisible dot as a magical doorway to wherever and to places and destinations unknown.

While Cameron, the world traveler, found the happening somewhat amusing, his insides still harbored a fear. Had he been asleep, did the possibility of his no longer being here exist? Could he have been eaten?

Cameron put the thought aside as outrageous but intended to revisit eventually. At this moment, he turned his attention to the flask which could have injured him.

## CHAPTER FIFTY

# THE FLASK

There it was, lying harmlessly, innocently, and silently on the floor next to the bed. "Just a flask. A simple, gooky covered, dripping and not too special flask." Cameron remarked softly to himself. That was all he had to do. If he had kept fully quiet, he would not have disturbed the spirit inhabiting the flask.

He did not keep quiet. Suddenly the lying down flask popped and up-righted itself in a loud snap. This immediately gained Cameron's full attention. This invading, apparently discarded piece of garbage with a spirit inside it, reacted immediately.

A not-so-soft bass voice came out of it. It said, "So you think I am not too special." The flask bounced and hit the floor making a clomping sound as it made its point. "Well, I must tell you off. First you need your facts before you come to conclusions. You have no facts, so your conclusions are wrong."

Cameron would ordinarily been amused, but not now. Somewhat puzzled he reflected on the event and thought to himself, "Here I am in my own bedroom. My door is closed. Then visualize that the ceiling opens, and a "mouth" essentially spits out of nowhere a discarded flask that is now scolding me. There is something wrong here."

"I want you to know that I have been traveling several thousand miles just to be here. I am not a flask. The flask is my means of transportation, nothing more. My country was overrun by malevolent dryads seeking an aggressive misdirected romantic, loving desire for my beautiful Thalian women who are like none other.

As King, I stood in their way, but I and my military were not able to protect my kingdom and many perished in the effort. I sought safety in this enchanted flask which, after it sealed itself, rose into the air and flying through space eventually drifted into a river. Now I am here both as the result of natural currents and the enchanted powers which swallowed me and my transport. It is now placing me before you, whoever you are. I have not the slightest idea as to why I stand before you except that I trust in the powers of my enchanted flask."

There was now silence. Not a word, not a sound except the sound of silence.

A puzzled Cameron spoke forcefully, the silence being cut like a lightning bolt.

"Well, well Mr. King yours is an interesting story if it's real." While Cameron was not loud, for a character change his voice was very authoritative.

Once again silence. The tired King kept a respectful and exhausted silence. He knew somehow that his journey brought him to safety. The Flask was enchanted to do only that: achieve safety.

The silence was deafening. The silence was broken by the flask increasing in size to that of a barrel and a half. It grew taller than Cameron's six-foot two frame. Astounded, Cameron stepped back and as he did, he could see an unseen door on the flask slide open.

Before Cameron stood a six foot ten, well-built muscular man bearing a golden crown on his head and a four-foot jeweled sword in his hands.

Cameron was wspeechless. He said mollified, "There are no words." Then once again for several moments there was only silence. Neither Cameron nor the King spoke.

The bedroom door opened. Standing there were Jim Henigson and the Spaceship alien Mrazy Xilx. Jim spoke first. Looking at Cameron, directly eye to eye and within eight inches, he asked in an inquisitive but solicitous tone, "Cameron, what have you done?"

Xilx just stood there simply observing the large flask and crowned King, the giant man, a stuttering Cameron and himself, an inquisitive Xilx and Henigson. It was Jack Henigson who carried the torch of investigation.

In this instance, Cameron was a true victim. He had absolutely no idea about what happened or why. After stuttering a bit, an almost broken-down Cameron explained, "I was finally at peace in my mind and happy. Then a hard to see small, small, small spot on the ceiling grew into a great mouth. The ceiling had not even one flaw except for that single small dot, not bigger than a pencil point. The disrespectful 'what-ever-it-was' even stuck a disrespectful tongue at me but then spat out this stained, tarnished, saliva and mucous covered, banged-up, dented flask almost at my head, as if it had been aimed!

Incredibly, as though out of nowhere, this miserable small flask engaged me in conversation, like I really did not need or want conversation at all especially with a talking flask!

I thought and wondered, "is there no one else here?" Then I had a conversation with only the then diminutive, small flask, there was no one else about, or so I thought.

Then this sword-armed, crowned giant came out of a now extra-large expanded flask with an incredible story."

Cameron stopped and needed to sit down before he passed out. The entire episode exhausted him mostly because of his fear of being gobbled up by the ceiling, a growing and conversing flask, an armed, crowned giant, all in his supposedly private, secure and secluded bedroom was just too much for him at this time. He found a chair and just dropped into it. Plop!

Mrazy Xilx now entered the conversation. "Jack and I both gathered some broken up mental telepathy from Cameron. Although we wanted to wait until we could make some sense of what was going on, we decided it was time to investigate directly as we heard more than just one voice. I'm glad we did."

"What you say, Cameron is truly incredible. It is apparently not your doing. There is more here than meets the eye. A question is 'why did this flask seek you specifically, or accidentally? Who is this King? It is obvious he IS a king. From 'where' is yet another question. An even better question is from WHEN?'"

Jack and Mrazy, being a bit distant from the immediate happening, were more levelheaded than either Cameron or the King. They were both solicitous.

Jack asked the King if he'd like to have a glass of water and a chair.

The King answered "Yes, thank you."

He was quickly accommodated and served.

He needed a pitcher of water, and it was provided. The King explained that when he escaped the invasion, he also took his daughter with him. The King could not go without the daughter he was protecting.

She hid in the Flask.

The King turned around and extended his hand into the Flask.

His daughter, Princess Cinika, took his hand and came out of the flask, also exhausted and thirsty and she was also provided with water.

Jack led them both to the extra bedroom which held two double beds.

Mrazy and Jack both understood that the stress, exhaustion of the two, now "guests" in the Henigson Household, needed rest as well as drink.

Fortunately, Jack's house had more rooms and invited the King to follow him to the separate bedroom.

Jack, as a gracious host, saw that these uninvited guests were comfortable. Jack was full of wonder, but at this late hour rest is what is needed by all. Questions would have to wait a wakened mind and new energy.

Jack was perplexed about these strangers, the safety of his home's residents, and most puzzling was about how they were able to understand each other's language.

## Chapter Fifty-One

# KING EDYVAARD

A new day, two very strange new house guests. Minds were now awake, and energy recharged. Interest abounded. Jack wondered along with Mr. Xilx about from where these strangers came. How they spoke and understood each other was still another wonder. Why the strange dress. Moreover, the strange transport. Why was it enchanted? More importantly, why was it here and inside Jack's house and in Cameron's bedroom, via a yawning mouthed ceiling? Indeed!

Questions abounded. The King arose at dawn, along with the rising sun. Princess Cinika also arose. They both sought their hosts who still slumbered but did not wish to disturb them. They both quietly examined the surroundings, which they found both strange and yet familiar. There was something mystic about them beyond what was already known and revealed by last night's occurrences.

What was revealed had even more to reveal. It was not enough. Jack and Xilx aroused themselves from the night's mantle and were very surprised to find their strange guests not only pert, inquisitive and exploring the environment of their house and their outdoor greenery but also fully dressed in the fineries of a King and robes of a Princess even though they arrived with no luggage.

The questions would wait until breakfast was over. Served were coffee, milk, orange juice and oatmeal. The King and Princess accepted what was offered without question and gratefully. They were introduced to each item and consumed each with gusto.

King Edyvaard mistakenly believed that he was still in his own homeland. He had no knowledge of the thousands of miles away from his kingdom he had travelled. He had no idea about the amount of time that passed. The King mistakenly explained their presence from nowhere using an assumption that they did not travel very far.

The King began, "I believe you would like to know about us, my Princess and myself. Prepare for the unbelievable as the truth. We are from right here. We have lived here all our lives as have our people.

Many centuries ago, we occupied this very same land, this very same place. Although my Princess Cinika and I are alive it is only through the spell of our learned wizard that we survive the millennia between our time and now. The creation and development of the transporter Flask provided all our needs. Our people and my Queen have perished millennia past and for both me and the Princess it is still fresh in our minds. The love we had is the love we still have both for our queen, our people and each other.

We did not live as you apparently do today. Disease, pestilence and warfare were constant plagues during our lives. I hope it is not like that here.

I notice running water and by some conjuring, you also have some of which is hot, of all unbelievable things. But enough of that. Then you have that round bowl with a lid. That is confusing because you have another higher round bowl with no lid. We need your instructions and as to what are their differences.

You also should be wondering how it is that we can communicate with you and vice-versa. Simply put, it was the spell our wizard placed on us. The same spell which permits our communication also allowed us to enter a large room with all our millennial needs supplied and then have it shrink to the size of a wine bottle or Flask. It was good that it was made of metal. That helped it to both float and our occupancy to survive safely over the many intervening years.

Its metal exterior disguised it, and we were set afloat in both prevailing winds and floating in the currents of the river wherever it might have been. We would both float on the waters wherever they were and fly on the winds as the situation for our security was part of the enchantment qualification and required us to then land only if the place contained safety.

If there were no safety, we would not be able to leave the transporter and we would not be able to leave La Bocca della Verità, our spiritual transporter. Should the location not be safe we would not be released.

We could tell that the passage of millennia encouraged La Bocca della Verità to evict us considering the force by which we were expelled!

The spell would cause us to be spat out only at a place where safety exists, no matter how long or how distant both regarding space and time. As is said in your culture, 'This is the Spot!' and we were forcefully evicted after several thousands of years!

Even though that transporter shrunk on the outside its internal size did not. We were not cramped for space at all. Now we are stranded and seek asylum here, wherever this is."

# CHAPTER FIFTY-TWO

# LA BOCCA DE LA VERITÀ

**M**r. Xilx questioned King Edyvaard: What is this La Bocca Della Verità? It sounds familiar to me, but it and its actions are still strange.

The King replied "It dates back to the first century of Roman Times. I was King of a nearby land and I knew of it. All Kings of different lands in the area knew of it. In matters of truth or lies, La Bocca De La Verità would be the final decision for or against the accused.

Should the accused wish to conclusively prove his innocence all he had to do would be to place his hand in the mouth of the Bocca and swear away. What made the testimony of the accused true or false would be if true, nothing would happen. If false, the stone mouth would close and the accused would lose his hand, thus proving guilt. Very few would dare to take a chance!"

The King let out a short laugh.

He knew very few, if any, people would dare to take that chance. Not only because the legend might be true but because there may be some error in their statement could cause them the loss of a hand. La Bocca de la Verità had very few takers, ever.

All those in the room were suddenly very silent. Not a sound.

Because of broadcast mental telepathy, late arrival Henry also now joined the scene. Very respectfully Henry was there to hear the King's report and was also silent. The group was stunned into a humble silence.

They all realized that before them stood very special and unique people from more than two thousand years in the past! Why the spirit of La Bocca saw a location containing Cameron Schulz's bedroom as a "safe" place puzzled each of them.

Not one of them saw anything about the "original" Cameron as safe. Perhaps in the future, maybe so, but it was still too soon. A "safe" Cameron was not yet proven. Passage of time and confluence of good deeds from Cameron alone was needed to prove it.

The passage of time will reveal all.

# EPILOGUE

Although the DESE group has found the cause and eliminated their sleepless nights and the unexplained thefts in various parts of the world as well, DESE members have yet to learn the full extent of the gifts and secrets of Cameron Schultz's abilities.

They really do not know how to control Cameron and how to keep him on the straight and narrow path of good and legal. The release of Cameron into their DESE organization was only arrived at by the exact realization that his abilities exceeded the abilities of the gifted ones in the DESE organization, at least for the present time. The question of Cameron, his ideals and integrity, is currently an unopened box, perhaps something like Pandora's where all the evil in the world is permitted to escape to plague everyone, everywhere.

The adventure with Cameron has just begun. Xilx and Elizabeth have not revealed all their abilities to the DESE group either. Although they appear and act human, they are aliens. They will most likely achieve a greater revelation of Cameron's true nature.

Life is both a living and a learning experience. The future is always unknown.

Now enters the King with a kingdom adjacent to the Roman Empire and a trader with King Herod. He knew of the man who raised the dead, cured the lepers, made the lame to walk and the blind to see. King Edyvaard regretted that he never got to meet him. He believed he could have used his help in so many ways for humankind and himself.

We discover it day by day and minute to minute. There is much to learn of Cameron Schultz and only time will tell!

# ADDENDA F.Y.I.

Wikipedia Quote: The **Institute of <u>Noetic</u> <u>Sciences</u>** (IONS) was co-founded in 1973 by former astronaut <u>Edgar Mitchell</u> and investor <u>Paul N. Temple</u> to encourage and conduct research on human potentials. Institute programs include "extended human capacities," "integral health and healing", and "emerging worldviews."

This research includes topics such as:

<u>spontaneous remission</u>, <u>meditation</u>, <u>consciousness</u>, <u>alternative healing</u> practices, <u>spirituality</u>, <u>human potential</u>, <u>psychic abilities</u> and <u>survival of consciousness after bodily death</u>.

Headquartered outside <u>Petaluma, California</u>, the organization is situated on a 200-<u>acre</u> (80 <u>hectare</u>) campus that includes offices, a research laboratory, and a retreat center (originally the campus of <u>World College West</u>). The institute does not grant educational degrees.

For your information, Google
"QUANTUM ENTANGLEMENT"

For your enlightenment place these on the internet URL and watch.

<u>http://www.youtube.com/watch?v=7Acgvjw2s5k</u>

<u>http://www.youtube.com/watch?v=l-pY3OehTLI</u>

http://www.youtube.com/watch?v=OwlH36M34Xo

# MEET THE AUTHOR

Christopher A. Salvo grew up in Mamaroneck and Purchase, New York and graduated from White Plains, N.Y. High School, attended the University of Michigan and the Columbia University School of Dental and Oral Surgery on a competitive New York State Regents Scholarship. He and his wife, Cyndy, son Philip, and daughter Valerie live in Connecticut. His additional four children are married with son Frank in Emerald Isle, N,C., Matthew in Rincon, PR, daughter Katharine in Chicago, IL and daughter Christina living in Minneapolis, MN. His son, Matthew is the model on the cover of this book.

Christopher is an avid writer of magical, quasi-scientific fantasy fiction and is expected to be quite prolific.

His e-mail address is *christopherasalvo@gmail.com.*

# Henry, Black Lightning and Murphy's Law
## CHRISTOPHER A. SALVO

**High School teenager helps the U.S. Government to Solve Mysterious Fort Knox Gold Thefts Using Magical Skills in Magical and Fantasy Adventure**

Henry, a high school 17-year-old uses his extraordinary abilities to help the United States preserve its secure gold vaults.

Christopher A. Salvo uses the newest of science fiction with mystery and fantasy in an unusual adventure involving international police work and the secret federal ***Department of Extraordinary Situations and Events*** abbreviated as "**DESE**".

This book is a continuation of "Henry, Black Lightning and the Rubber Band" and continues some of the earlier characters but introduces Cameron Schultz, a magically gifted thief as well as being a conflicted beneficent individual. The story centers on the mental treasures of Henry, and fellow DESE agents, some from Area 51 as well as aliens and mythical creatures.

Henry is mentally assaulted and suffers sleepless headaches and nights along with his mental telepathic associates. They all share in Henry's discomfort. As a result, they all join him in solving the national mystery from Kentucky to Washington, DC, Greenwich, CT and San Francisco, CA.

Everyone will dive headlong into this imaginative story loaded with engaging characters.

www.ingramcontent.com/pod-product-compliance
Lightning Source LLC
Chambersburg PA
CBHW071417300726
48976CB00004B/1156